A FIGURE IN HIDING

A blind peddler's warning and a weird glass eye plunge Frank and Joe Hardy into one of the most baffling cases they have ever tackled.

The young detectives' investigation takes them to a walled estate guarded by savage dogs, where a wealthy businessman is hiding out in fear of his life. Later, a midnight telephone tip leads to a strange encounter on a lonesome hillside—and a hair-raising escape from death at the bottom of Barmet Bay.

The theft of a valuable Oriental idol called the Jeweled Siva, a daringly designed hydrofoil speedboat the *Sea Spook,* the strange disappearance at sea of a prime suspect, and a walking mummy all figure excitingly in this complex case.

In a climax that will hold the reader spellbound with suspense, Frank and Joe find themselves trapped in a sinister house of mystery from which there seems to be no escape!

"Signals are coming over this glass eye!"

Hardy Boys Mystery Stories

A FIGURE
IN
HIDING

BY

FRANKLIN W. DIXON

NEW YORK
GROSSET & DUNLAP
Publishers

CONTENTS

CHAPTER   PAGE

I	A Blind Lead	1
II	Trouble on the Wire	12
III	The Gatepost Eye	20
IV	Muscle Man	28
V	The River Spy	36
VI	Oriental Curse	44
VII	Beach Battle	52
VIII	DZ 7—	60
IX	A Cruise in the *Sea Spook*	69
X	Dangerous Dobermans	78
XI	A Midnight Deal	87
XII	Doom Ride!	95
XIII	Airport Vigil	103
XIV	Sinister Flower Gift	112
XV	The Brass Crescent	120
XVI	The Walking Mummy	127
XVII	Secret Signals	138
XVIII	News of a Racket	145
XIX	The Figure at the Window	154
XX	Mystery Madhouse	165

CHAPTER I

A Blind Lead

EXCITED fans were still milling about the Bayport High athletic field as the Hardy boys came out of the dressing room after their team's post-season win over the Alumni All-Stars.

"Great pitching, Frank!" a schoolmate yelled. "You really bore down in the clutches!"

Dark-haired, eighteen-year-old Frank Hardy grinned and waved. "Don't think that double of Joe's with the bases loaded didn't help!"

As the boys reached the street, a blind peddler approached them. He was wearing dark glasses and tapping a white cane. "Buy a pencil, please?" he mumbled.

Joe Hardy, blond and a year younger than his brother, fished in his pocket for a coin and dropped it into the man's tin cup.

"Thank you, sir!" The peddler pressed a pencil and a small white card into Joe's hand as the boys hurried past him toward their red convertible, parked several yards up the street.

Joe glanced at the card as they were climbing into the car. "Hey! What's this?"

"What's what?"

"Take a look. The blind man gave it to me."

Frank's joking smile changed to a bewildered frown as he studied the card. It bore the picture of a human eye and a printed plea for better eye care from a national health society.

The picture had pencil marks over it. The pupil had been changed to a catlike oval shape with zigzag spark lines radiating from it. Some of the words in the printed heading had been crossed out:

WATCH OUT

FOR THE FIRST SIGNS OF

BAD EYESIGHT!

Frank turned the card over. Scribbled in pencil on the blank side was the notation: *Tell FH!*

" 'FH' must mean Dad!" Frank exclaimed.

Fenton Hardy, the boys' father, had been an ace detective on the New York City police force before he retired to the coastal town of Bayport and became a famous private investigator.

"But what about those crossed-out words?" Joe queried. "This way, it reads 'Watch out for bad eye!' "

"Let's try to find that blind man!" Frank suggested.

The boys dashed back down the street, but the peddler was already lost to view among the throng outside the field. Frank and Joe circled the block without catching sight of him.

"I'll bet he's one of Dad's underworld informers," Frank stated. "He didn't want to be seen talking to us, so he got lost in a hurry."

"That's probably the answer," Joe agreed as the boys headed back to their parked car. "But if the peddler was so afraid of being spotted, why didn't he phone his message?"

"Maybe he tried and got no answer, so he tracked us down. Let's go home and see if Dad's back from his trip yet."

Frank and Joe hopped into their car and Frank drove off.

Two blocks farther on, as they stopped for the traffic light, a truck owned by the Prito Construction Company pulled up alongside. Tony Prito, a lanky, black-haired school chum, was at the wheel.

"How'd the game come out?" he called.

"Frank handcuffed 'em! Three-nothing shutout!" Joe waved his clasped hands in a victory sign.

"Nice going! Wish I could've seen it!" As Tony shifted gears to start up again, he added, "If you fellows want to see something pretty, take a spin out on the bay. Bill Braxton has his *Sea Spook* on a shakedown run."

"Hey! That'd be worth watching," Joe said.

Frank toed the accelerator. "Maybe we can catch it if we hurry."

The *Sea Spook*, a new, rakish hydrofoil craft, was the talk of Barmet Bay. Bill Braxton, a young mechanic and stock-car racing driver, had designed and built it in his spare time.

A few minutes later the convertible turned up the driveway of the Hardys' pleasant, tree-shaded house. Frank and Joe leaped out and bounded up the front steps. The door was locked. Frank quickly opened it with his key.

"Anyone home?" he called. His voice echoed emptily through the house.

"I guess Mother and Aunt Gertrude aren't back from that bazaar yet," Joe said. "We can leave a note for Dad."

He hurried to the hallway telephone stand and began jotting a message on the memo pad.

"Tell him we'll be out in our boat so he can call us," Frank suggested. "Then we can give him the details over our radio." The Hardy boys' motorboat, the *Sleuth*, was equipped with a powerful marine transceiver.

After pausing in the kitchen for glasses of milk and a handful of cookies, the brothers locked up and headed in the convertible for the Bayport waterfront. As they rolled along through the hot June sunshine, Joe flicked on the dashboard radio. A newscaster was saying:

"A daring robbery in New York City last night

netted thieves a small Oriental idol called the Jeweled Siva, valued at over twenty thousand dollars. The owner of the art curio shop from which it was taken said the ivory figure stood only six inches high but was studded with valuable gems."

"Wow! That's some haul!" Joe murmured. "I wouldn't mind working on a case like that."

The two boys, who had inherited their father's zest for crime puzzles, had already solved a number of baffling mysteries starting with *The Tower Treasure.* On one of their most challenging cases, *The Sinister Signpost,* they had restored a stolen race horse to its owner.

When they reached the waterfront, Frank pulled into a parking lot and the brothers strode off toward the Hardy boathouse. In a few minutes the *Sleuth* was knifing through the harbor toward open water.

Joe grinned in delight at the feel of their boat leaping along through the waves. Frank was scanning the blue expanse of the bay through binoculars. Presently he picked out a fast-moving hull that was throwing up plumes of spray.

"There's the *Sea Spook!* Man, look at that baby go!"

Joe gunned the *Sleuth.* Soon it was close enough for them to view the *Sea Spook* clearly without the glasses. The hydrofoil was streaking over the surface at a speed that made the boys' eyes pop.

"She must be doing fifty knots!" Joe gasped.

The *Spook's* hull stood well above the waves, on struts connected to her curved foils. They were planing along through the water.

"Watch your course!" Frank cautioned Joe.

The *Sea Spook* began to execute a graceful figure eight, so tightly and smoothly that the Hardys could scarcely believe their eyes. It rounded the final turn, then headed seaward again.

Joe opened the throttle wide, trying not to lose the other craft, but it sped off. "It's hopeless!" he groaned.

A moment later the hydrofoil reversed course again. Apparently its pilot was going to do another figure eight. This time, the execution was not nearly so smooth.

Frank snatched up the binoculars. "That's not Braxton at the wheel," he reported. "He turned it over to another fellow."

The new pilot was sweeping a much wider curve that brought the *Sea Spook* almost abeam of the *Sleuth*. He closed the top half of the eight so erratically that Joe was taken by surprise.

"Look out!" Frank yelled. "We're on a collision course!"

The hydrofoil was bearing down on the *Sleuth* at blinding speed. Joe glimpsed two frantic faces at the cabin window. Frank could see Braxton pushing his shipmate aside to take over as Joe swerved the *Sleuth* hard a-starboard.

In the nick of time, the *Sea Spook* banked to port. But the turn threw up a sheet of spray that hit the *Sleuth* like the slap of a giant hand. Already heeling, the motorboat turned turtle and both boys were thrown into the water!

Frank and Joe swam to the surface, gasping and blinking. The hydrofoil's hull was slowly settling into the waves as Braxton reduced speed. He brought the craft around and halted it near the Hardys. Then he dashed out of the cabin to the open afterdeck, his passenger at his heels, to haul Frank and Joe aboard. In a few moments they stood on deck.

"Are you okay?" Bill Braxton asked anxiously. He was a tanned, muscular young man, wearing a seaman's jersey and faded dungarees.

"Sure. No harm done," said Frank. "Just soaked to the skin. Good thing it's such a hot day."

Braxton started to apologize for the accident, but the man with him interrupted. "What in blazes is wrong with you punks?" he stormed at the Hardys. "Haven't you got brains enough to keep out of the way? This thing isn't a paddle boat, you know!"

Joe's quick temper flared. "A paddle boat's all you should handle, mister!" he retorted.

"Relax, Joe," Frank cut in. "We probably did

come closer than we should have. Got too interested in watching, I guess."

"Let's all forget it," Braxton said hastily. "We'd
better do something about your boat."

He maneuvered the *Sea Spook* close to the
Sleuth and helped the brothers right it. But the
motorboat had shipped too much water to be used
again immediately, so a towline was attached and
the hydrofoil started back to port.

"By the way," Braxton told his passenger,
"these two boys are Frank and Joe Hardy. Their
dad's a famous detective. Maybe you've heard of
him. . . . Boys, meet Mr. Lambert."

The man gave a surly grunt. Frank and Joe nodded coolly. Lambert was about forty, with a gaunt, hard-looking face that seemed strangely pale. His long, thin nose was slightly crooked, as if it had once been broken.

On the way into the harbor, the Hardys asked Bill numerous questions about his interesting

craft. He explained that as it got up speed, the water exerted an upward lift on the foils, just like air on the wings of a plane.

"Is this an ocean-going job?" Joe asked.

"Sure, except that it jolts a bit in heavy seas," Braxton replied. "Most designers use submerged foils for that type of service, but I've worked out ones that are pretty smooth."

He added that Mr. Lambert was interested in buying the craft and that today's run had been a demonstration.

After they had pulled alongside the dock, Lambert said curtly, "I'll get in touch with you later, Braxton." He picked up his sports jacket which had been flung on one of the seats, put it on, and scrambled up the dock ladder.

"Nice guy," Joe muttered. "Not even a thank-you for the ride!"

Bill grinned wryly. "He's a possible customer, so I had to be nice to him. Actually, it was his fault your boat got swamped. He froze at the wheel."

"I know—I saw you take over," Frank said. As he spoke, Frank saw something glittering on the deck and stooped down to pick it up. "Say, is Lambert blind in one eye?"

"Not that I know of. Why?"

"Someone dropped a glass eye. It isn't yours, is it?"

Braxton shook his head. "Good grief, no. That thing doesn't even look wearable!"

He stared at the object in puzzlement. So did Joe. It seemed larger than a glass eye should be and had a queer-shaped pupil with reddish vein lines radiating outward.

Suddenly Joe gasped. "Jumpin' catfish, Frank!" he exclaimed. "That looks just like the eye on the blind man's card!"

CHAPTER II

Trouble on the Wire

FRANK was startled. "You're right, Joe. The eye has the same oval-shaped pupil."

"And these veins are just like the spark lines penciled on the picture."

Braxton was mystified. "I suppose you two know what you're talking about," he said dryly, "but it makes no sense to me."

The Hardys grinned. Frank explained briefly about the blind peddler's card. Then he asked if the young mechanic knew Lambert's address.

"No, and he doesn't live in Bayport," Braxton replied. "He came here just to see the *Spook*. I believe he's staying at the Bayview Motel."

"Joe and I will take the glass eye there and see if it's his," Frank said.

The Hardys changed into swimming trunks, which they got from their car, then wrung out their drenched clothing and spread it to dry while they bailed out the *Sleuth*. By the time they were ready to start for home, the boys looked fairly presentable again.

"Good thing this wash-and-wear stuff dries so fast," Joe said, "or we'd get a lecture from Aunt Gertrude."

Frank chuckled. "She'd have us turning blue with pneumonia, and then bawl us out for going near such a crazy contraption as the *Sea Spook!*"

The boys parked in the Hardy driveway and hurried into the house. Their pretty mother and tall, angular Aunt Gertrude Hardy had returned. Mrs. Hardy informed her sons that their father had sent a telegram saying he would not return home until the next morning.

Aunt Gertrude, though strict, was very fond of her nephews and always interested in the mysteries they were solving. "What's that card you boys left on the telephone stand?" she asked.

"Oh, nothing very important," Frank said, his eyes twinkling. "It's just something a peddler gave us for Dad."

"Humph." Aunt Gertrude pursed her lips.

The boys smothered grins, knowing she had already gleaned as much from Joe's note and was curious to know more.

Mrs. Hardy laughed. "Now stop teasing, you two," she admonished.

"Oh, it doesn't matter, Laura," her sister-in-law said airily, and started for the kitchen.

Frank and Joe followed her and related the whole episode of the blind peddler.

"The fellow probably spotted a one-eyed murderer in town," Miss Hardy said. "In fact, the killer may be after him and he wants your father to rescue him."

The boys became serious. "Honestly, Aunty," Joe said soothingly, "we did pick up a clue. It's sort of gruesome."

Curiosity overcame Miss Hardy. "I don't scare easily. Show it to me."

Joe took out a folded clean handkerchief and unwrapped it, disclosing the glass eye. Aunt Gertrude gasped, but quickly demanded, "Where did you get that?"

When Frank explained, Aunt Gertrude wagged her head. "This is a sinister omen. You two be careful."

After supper the boys drove to the Bayview Motel. The manager, a fat, balding man, shook his head when they inquired for Lambert.

"Sorry, boys. You just missed him. He checked out not more'n fifteen minutes ago." The manager frowned. "Certainly looked upset."

"How come?" Joe asked.

"Search me. When he stopped in after dinner and told me to get his bill ready, he looked calm enough. Then about half an hour later when he came to check out, he was red in the face and acted sore at something. Kind o' worried, too."

"Maybe he got a disturbing phone call," Frank suggested.

Again the manager shook his head. "No—if he'd had a call, I'd know it because they all come through this switchboard here."

Frank explained that he and Joe were the sons of Fenton Hardy, the private investigator, and asked if Lambert had left any forwarding address.

The manager leafed through the card file of registrations. "No. He left that space on his card blank."

The boys thanked him and walked out. As they drove away, Frank said, "When Lambert went to pack, he may have discovered he'd lost the glass eye. That could be what upset him."

"Maybe," Joe agreed. "But so what?"

"He may go back to Braxton's boathouse to find out if he dropped it on the *Sea Spook*."

"Hey, that's an idea! Step on it, Frank!"

"There's an easier way." Frank swung off the road toward a hamburger drive-in. "I'll give Bill a ring. He's probably still tinkering."

Setting the brake, Frank jumped out of the convertible and hurried to the small building. He thumbed through a directory, then dialed the number on a pay telephone. Braxton answered.

"Bill, this is Frank Hardy. Has that fellow Lambert been back to your boathouse asking for the glass eye?"

"Lambert? No. I haven't seen him. Why?"

Frank hastily explained.

"You want me to stall him if he shows up, eh?"
Bill said. "Okay, Frank, I'll—"

Braxton's voice broke off with a groan. There
was a crashing noise as if the phone had fallen
from his hand. A moment later came a click.
Frank jiggled the hook frantically, but the line
was dead.

He dashed out to the convertible and told Joe
how the call had been cut short.

"What do you suppose happened?" Joe asked.

"I don't know—but someone hung up and I
doubt if it was Bill!"

Frank sent the car roaring out of the lot. As
it sped back into Bayport, the summer evening
traffic seemed even worse than usual. Three red
lights in a row left both boys fuming with im-
patience at the delay.

When they finally reached the waterfront,
Frank parked and they ran to Braxton's boathouse. The shedlike structure extended over the
water on piles. The dockside door was unlocked.
The brothers burst in and gasped when they saw
the young mechanic sprawled face down near his
desk. Frank reached him first.

"Is he alive?" Joe murmured fearfully.

"Still breathing." Frank fingered Braxton's
scalp. "There's a big lump on the back of his
head. Someone must have sneaked up and conked
him while he was talking to me."

The Hardys noticed signs of a hasty search. Desk drawers had been yanked open and ransacked. Blueprints lay scattered about.

"Bill's attacker wanted something pretty bad," Joe remarked. "I wonder if it was that glass eye."

Using a handkerchief so as not to smudge any fingerprints, Joe phoned the police and asked for an ambulance. Meanwhile, Frank was working on Braxton and soon revived him.

"You didn't see who hit you?" Frank asked.

Bill shook his head painfully. "It became stuffy in here so I opened the door. I suppose that's why I didn't hear the guy come in."

Beyond the working platform, the *Sea Spook* lay rocking gently in its berth, enclosed by a wooden walkway on each side. The Hardys went aboard and saw that Braxton's storage lockers in the cabin also had been rifled.

A police car and an ambulance soon arrived. The intern insisted that Braxton be taken to the hospital for X-rays and observation. The police then took charge, and the boys went home. No report came during the evening and finally the brothers went to bed.

Next morning when Frank and Joe came down to breakfast, they found their father already at the table. Fenton Hardy, a tall, big-shouldered man, greeted his sons with a grin.

"When did you get back, Dad?" Joe asked eagerly.

"Flew in about an hour ago. I hear you fellows had some excitement yesterday."

"It was pretty grim," Frank said. He and Joe gave their father all the facts.

Mr. Hardy had the blind man's card on the table near his plate. "This must have come from Zatta," he remarked. "Henry Zatta."

"One of your regular informers?" Frank asked.

"Yes, he picks up a good many underworld tips for me. In fact, he's an ex-con himself."

"He must have heard our names and spotted us as your sons," Joe said. "That is, if his blindness is phony."

Fenton Hardy nodded. "It's partly an act, although he *is* missing one eye."

Frank and Joe exchanged glances, then Joe excused himself to hurry out to the boys' laboratory over the garage. He brought the glass eye back to the table. "Could this be Zatta's?"

Mr. Hardy studied it, then shook his head. "Too large and grotesque to be wearable. . . . Hmm. This eye business may have something to do with the Goggler gang. They wear spectacles with bulging eyes on all their— Say, wait! Did you say Lambert had a crooked nose?"

"That's right," Frank answered. "Why?"

"Sounds like a hoodlum named Spotty Lemuel."

As soon as the Hardys finished breakfast, the boys accompanied their father to his study. He leafed quickly through his criminal file and soon produced a photograph.

"That's Lambert, all right!" Joe exclaimed. "No wonder he's called Spotty. His face here is covered with freckles."

Mr. Hardy nodded. "He probably had them bleached off by a dermatologist." The detective suggested that the boys try to locate Zatta, since he himself would be busy on a new case. Joe asked hopefully if this had anything to do with the theft of the Jeweled Siva. Mr. Hardy said No, saying he had been engaged to run down a swindler named Pampton.

Soon afterward, as Mr. Hardy left the house, Frank called the hospital and learned that Bill Braxton was better. A moment later the doorbell rang loud and long.

"Sufferin' cats! Who's that?" said Joe.

The boys went to answer it. A startling sight greeted them. Their visitor was a thin old man with a hearing aid. Bare from the waist up, he wore Bermuda shorts and a floppy straw hat and carried a Malacca cane.

"Out of my way, boy!" Nudging Frank aside with his cane, he rushed in and rasped, "Quick! Shut the door! They're after me!"

Frank looked out in astonishment. "There's no one after you—just a station wagon cruising along the street."

With a moan, the old man fainted.

CHAPTER III

The Gatepost Eye

FRANK and Joe carried the old man to the living-room sofa.

"Who in the world is he?" said Joe.

"And who was after him?" Frank added.

Hearing the commotion, Mrs. Hardy and Aunt Gertrude came from the kitchen. Both women gasped in alarm at sight of the old man, who was breathing heavily.

Mrs. Hardy felt his pulse and Aunt Gertrude said, "Get some water."

As Frank hastily brought a glass, the man began to revive. With one of his bony hands he fumbled in a pocket of his shorts and plucked out a bottle of pills.

"Sh-sh-shake me out t-two, son."

Frank obeyed and the old man gulped them down. Presently his color returned and he struggled to sit up. Aunt Gertrude attempted to make him comfortable, but the old man yanked the sofa cushion from her hand.

"Leave me alone, woman!" He added in a mutter, "Confounded females! Just like my daughter! I wouldn't be in this fix if she hadn't shanghaied me to that blasted farm!"

"You're very independent," Laura Hardy said with a smile.

The elderly man glared at her. Then, as she continued to smile, a twinkle came into his watery blue eyes and he cackled, "Yes, I am. But I can see that doesn't impress *you*."

Glancing out the window, Frank saw the station wagon cruise past again. The gold lettering on it read: DOC GRAFTON'S HEALTH FARM. He remembered hearing of the place—a luxurious resort overlooking Barmet Bay where older men of means came to regain their health.

"Say, is that where you're staying?" Frank asked. "Doc Grafton's Health Farm?"

The man's face darkened with wrath. "Doc Grafton's Vegetable Farm they *should* call it—or loony bin! Figured I'd go loony myself if I had to sit around there listening to my arteries harden. So I sneaked off."

The man snorted and fished a large cigar from his pocket. He unwrapped it, bit off the tip, and lit the cigar with a gold lighter.

"You say you sneaked away from the health farm?" Joe asked.

"Uh-huh. Had my chauffeur meet me outside. Then some fellow down at the harbor told me to get in touch with the Hardy boys. . . . You two *are* the Hardy boys, I presume?"

"Yes, sir." Frank introduced everyone, and the old man explained that he was Zachary Mudge, a financier and businessman from New York.

"My daughter and her husband claimed I needed a rest," Mudge went on, "so like a fool I let 'em ship me down here to this vegetable farm. Claimed I'd have a heart attack if I didn't stay away from that stock-market ticker tape." The elderly man's bushy gray eyebrows shot up. "Which reminds me! Have to call my broker! You, boy"—waving to Joe—"help me to the phone!"

Mrs. Hardy and Aunt Gertrude retired to the kitchen while Frank and Joe waited for their eccentric visitor to make the call. Finally he returned to the living room, contentedly trailing clouds of smoke.

As he sat down, Aunt Gertrude marched into the hall. She flung open the front door and stood vigorously fanning the hall air. Mudge grinned merrily and took another deep puff.

"You—er—were saying that you wanted to get in touch with us, sir," Frank reminded him.

"Oh, yes. About that—what did you call it?— hydrofoil." Mr. Mudge explained that he had watched the *Sea Spook* through binoculars the day before, and had heard several people talking about it. "Looks to me like the coming thing for water travel—maybe a good investment opportunity."

He explained that he had had his chauffeur drive him to the waterfront to talk to the craft's designer. But someone near the boathouse had told him about the assault on Braxton and advised him to see the Hardys. Mudge said he had looked up their address and told his chauffeur to drive him to their house.

"Then I noticed that health-farm station wagon on our tail—somebody at the place must have spotted me leaving. I slipped out of the car when we stopped for a traffic light and hoofed it the rest of the way." The elderly tycoon grimaced. "Guess I overdid things a bit."

"Bill Braxton is still in the hospital," Frank said. "We called just before you got here. But he should be out in a day or two. By the way, another man is interested in the *Sea Spook*."

"What's that?" Mudge stiffened, his eyes glinting suspiciously. "Who is he?"

"He gave his name as Lambert," Frank said.

Mudge scowled. "Never heard of him."

At this point, a limousine pulled up in front of the house. Zachary Mudge explained that he had ordered his chauffeur to pick him up here.

"Appreciate your help, boys."

They grinned. "Glad to give it."

As soon as Mudge had gone, Frank and Joe drove off in search of Henry Zatta. They cruised back and forth through Bayport without catching sight of the pseudo-blind man.

"Dad did say he works in other towns along the coast," Frank reminded Joe.

"Right. Let's try Ocean City next."

A couple of miles outside the town limits of Bayport they sighted a pudgy figure in a heavy sweat suit jogging alongside the road.

Joe gasped. "Don't tell me that's Chet Morton!"

"Working out off-season, too!" Frank chuckled. "Boy, now we've seen everything!"

Although Chet made a good lineman on the Bayport eleven, he was not noted for his physical activity. Chet's chief hobbies were food and relaxation whenever he had a chance.

The Hardys pulled up and their chum stopped to greet them. His moonface was lobster red and dripping with perspiration. Chet pulled out one end of the thick towel draped around his neck and mopped his forehead.

"You out of your mind?" Joe teased. "I thought you'd engaged a hammock for the summer."

"I'm getting in shape," Chet retorted. Plopping himself down on a boulder, he plucked out a candy bar, peeled off the wrapper, and began munching it hungrily.

"That chocolate bar will put you in shape,"

Frank said with a grin, "like a lead balloon."

"Aw, cut it out! I have to have some quick energy, don't I?"

"Listen, what's this roadwork all about?" Joe asked. "You're not doing it for fun."

Chet looked smug. "Just wait and see, wise guys. Certain people needed a powerfully built young fellow for an important athletic post, and I was their natural choice."

"Choice for what?" Joe gibed. "A before-and-after model for one of those diet ads?"

"Okay, pal. Have your laugh." Chet got up, and this time set off at a brisker pace.

The Hardys grinned and drove on. They spent the day searching Ocean City and a number of other places but found no trace of Zatta. Finally they returned to Bayport for a late supper.

Just as they were leaving the table, the telephone rang and Joe answered. The caller was the manager of the Bayview Motel.

"That fellow Lambert just came back here and left a forwarding address for mail," the man said. "I thought you boys might want to know."

"We sure do!" Joe said eagerly. He copied down the address and was surprised when it turned out to be a street on the outskirts of town. "Thanks a lot."

Joe showed the address to Frank. "Let's go see what Lambert—or Spotty Lemuel—has to say."

"Okay, but we'd better pass this information along to Chief Collig in case he wants to follow up on what happened to Bill Braxton."

Police Chief Collig was an old friend of the Hardys. After leaving a message for him with the police operator, Frank and Joe hurriedly started off in their convertible.

The address was on Malabar Road, a quiet street of old houses which were set well back from the pavement and screened by big trees and heavy shrubbery. Dusk had fallen as the boys cruised along slowly, aiming their spotlight at the house numbers. The one they sought—25—was visible in brass letters on a tall gate.

"Look!" Joe gasped, and Frank pulled over.

The spotlight glow revealed a large eye chalked on the gatepost!

In seconds the boys were out of the car. To their surprise, a FOR SALE sign was posted on the fence. The house looked dark.

"Apparently Lemuel hasn't moved in yet," Joe murmured. "But what about that eye?"

As the brothers walked to the gate, a figure moved on the front porch and came down the drive. He was a boy about sixteen—a wiry, cocky-looking youth in tight jeans and motorcycle boots.

He leaned on the gate and stared up and down at the Hardys with a mocking grin, his jaws chomping on a wad of gum. "Know what that means?" he said, pointing to the chalked eye.

"Maybe," Frank said evenly. "Who are you?"

"The checker, stupid. Who d'you suppose?" the boy retorted. "Look, are you guys here for the meeting or just snooping around?"

Joe glanced at his brother. "We're here for the meeting."

"Then let's see your pass." As the brothers hesitated, the youth pointed to the eye again and rasped, "Come on, don't try to con me. Have you got one or haven't you?"

On a sudden hunch, Frank took the glass eye from his pocket. The boy nodded. "Okay. Go on around to the back and knock twice."

As he spoke, he opened the gate. The Hardys entered and walked up the drive.

"Looks as though we made the grade!" Joe whispered triumphantly.

The boys' hearts were thumping as they went to the rear of the house. Here the weed-grown yard was shrouded in gloom. Joe was about to knock on the back door when Frank stopped him.

"What's the matter?"

"I don't know exactly, Joe, but there's something about this setup I don't—"

He broke off with a cry of alarm as two figures sprang at them out of the darkness! Both boys were seized and rough hands were clamped over their mouths!

CHAPTER IV

Muscle Man

THE brothers struggled wildly to break loose from the steely hands that clutched them and dug into their faces. As the two boys twisted around, they saw that the thugs were wearing nylon stocking masks drawn tightly over their heads.

Joe managed to brace himself long enough to deliver a stinging kick on the left shin of his foe. The man yelped with pain and loosened his hold. Joe promptly jerked his face free and let out a volley of piercing yells.

"Help! . . . Help! . . . Help!"

Frank's attacker was a thickset, barrel–chested brute. The man was scrabbling at Frank's pockets as if groping for the glass eye, which gave Frank an opportunity to wrench one arm loose. He swung a chopping right hook that caught his assailant on the side of the head.

Furious, the man let go of Frank and dealt him

a stunning backhand cuff that left the boy's right ear ringing. But Frank, too, was able to shout for help.

The Hardys' cries seemed to throw their attackers into a frenzy. Joe's opponent had tried to rip his pockets, but now bent all his efforts on silencing the youth. The other man clutched Frank's neck in his huge paws and tried to throttle his yells. The brothers fought back like wildcats, kicking, punching, and clawing.

Suddenly a police siren shrilled nearby. Brakes screeched to a halt and footsteps came pounding up the drive. The thugs hurled the boys aside and raced across the yard. Vaulting a back fence, they vanished into the night. Two policemen dashed up to Frank and Joe.

"They went that way!" Frank panted. "A couple of masked men!" The officers plunged in pursuit.

"Hey, Frank! Let's not forget that kid out front!" Joe exclaimed.

The boys ran around to the front of the house, but the "lookout" had disappeared. By now, neighbors' doors were opening and heads were popping out of windows along the street. The officers soon came running back.

One said to the Hardys, "Hop in with us and we may be able to nail those hoods before they get too far away."

Joe went with the driver while the other

policeman accompanied Frank in the convertible. On the way, each of the boys gave an account of what had happened and the police driver turned in a radio alarm.

Frank kept in touch with the prowl car via the Hardys' own two-way radio. The searchers sped up and down streets, crisscrossing the whole surrounding area. But after the officers had stopped to question a number of people, the pursuit was finally given up.

"How did you get to us so fast?" Joe asked the police driver.

"Chief Collig told us to go to 25 Malabar Road and pick up a man calling himself Lambert for questioning," the driver replied. "Some neighbor must have heard you two yelling, because we got another emergency call on the way."

The car returned to the scene of the attack and the policemen entered the house, using a strip of celluloid to open the door lock. The place proved to be empty. Frank and Joe were asked to accompany the two officers to police headquarters and report to the chief.

Collig, a big, grizzled veteran of the Bayport force, listened intently to the boys' story. "You think this whole caper was arranged by Spotty Lemuel, alias Lambert, to get hold of the glass eye?" he asked.

"Sure looks that way," Frank said. "Assuming he was the one who conked Bill Braxton, he must have heard enough of the phone conversation to guess that we had the eye. He also knew we were already looking for him, so he gave that phony address to the motel manager in hopes we'd fall for it."

Collig nodded. "That figures, all right." He asked to see the glass eye and studied it for a moment. "Any idea why Spotty's so eager to get this back?"

"Not yet," Frank said, "but Dad got a lead that may give us the answer. We'd like to hang on to the eye till we find out for sure."

"Okay. I'll have to admit it's got *me* stumped."

As the boys walked down the stone steps of headquarters, Frank said, "How about a milk-shake?"

Joe grinned. "You read my mind. I can sure use one!"

They drove several blocks to the Hot Rocket, a favorite eating spot of their high school crowd. A familiar yellow jalopy was parked outside.

"Well, well! Look who's in there!" Frank said.

The chunky figure of Chet Morton, the jalopy's owner, was seated in one of the booths. He was poring over a magazine and munching a hamburger.

"Hi, fellows!" he mumbled.

The Hardys gave their order and slid onto the seat across from him. Frank flipped up the cover of Chet's magazine and saw that it was *Muscle*

Man. A weight lifter with bulging arms and torso decorated the cover.

"Wow! You really are going in for physical culture!" Frank chuckled.

"And he-man food," Chet said, as the Hardys milkshakes were served. "That stuff you've got is for sissies. From now on, I'm sticking to ground beefsteak, milk, raw fruits, and leafy vegetables. No more candy."

He paused to flex a bicep and compare it to a photograph in the magazine.

"Boy, this is serious!" Joe said. "What's suddenly made you so hip on body-building?"

"Just for that wisecrack, I'll tell you," Chet said proudly. "Meet the new Assistant Supervisor of Physical Training at Doc Grafton's Health Farm!"

Frank and Joe stared in astonishment. "Assistant Supervisor of Physical Training!" Frank echoed. "Are you kidding?"

"Do I sound like it?" Chet bragged. "The chef there comes to our farm and buys all his vegetables. He told the doc about me and he offered me a job bouncing medicine balls to the guests and helping them work out. I start tomorrow morning."

Joe burst out laughing. "Now I get it. You mean they hired you as an exercise boy!"

Chet scowled. "Well . . . I'll be helping Doc Grafton train the people who come there, so

Assistant Supervisor is what the job amounts to. The doc used to be a real boxing trainer!"

Joe winked at his brother. "Can you picture Chet putting Zachary Mudge through the exercise bit?"

At Chet's puzzled look, the Hardys told him of their eccentric visitor. They also briefed him on their new mystery, ending with the recent attack on them.

The chubby boy whistled. "Glass eyes! Strong-arm crooks on the loose! Not for me!"

Frank grinned. "We may have to call on your muscles for help!"

"Oh, I'll be too busy for detective work," Chet said hastily. Although not eager to get involved in any dangerous situations, he had often joined the brothers in their sleuthing, and was a loyal friend.

"If you start tomorrow morning, Chet, how come you aren't home and asleep?" Frank asked. "Muscle men need their rest."

"Aw, I got roped into picking up Iola and Callie after the movie," Chet explained. "They went to the Bijou to see some creepy love picture."

The Hardys perked up. Joe liked Chet's sister, Iola, and her friend Callie Shaw was Frank's favorite date.

"Uh—look, old buddy," said Joe, "why don't you stay put and study some more valuable health tips? Frank and I can pick up the girls and bring them back here."

Chet looked up slyly. "Will you guys treat?"

"What a chiseler!" Frank groaned. "But okay."

"Then sure—go ahead."

"What time does the show let out?" Joe asked.

"Ten-fifteen," said Chet, and signaled the waiter for another hamburger.

Frank glanced at his wristwatch. "Twelve minutes. Let's scram, Joe."

The Bijou, a small neighborhood theater, closed its box office early and the marquee lights were already out. The Hardys found a parking spot down the street. Then they walked toward the theater.

As they approached it, a weird figure came dashing out the lobby. The man was clutching a tin box under one arm. His head was covered with a stocking mask. Over this was hooked a pair of comic-disguise glasses with bulging eyeballs that glowed in the dark!

"Good grief! Who's *that* nut?" Joe gasped.

Almost at the same moment came a scream from somewhere inside the lobby. The boys dashed forward just in time to see the woman cashier rush out of the office, waving her arms hysterically. "Stop him, someone!" she shrieked. "He's a thief!"

The masked man was already leaping into a car —a sleek, racy-looking blue hardtop. Before the

Hardys could reach him, the engine roared and the car shot away from the curb.

"That was one of the Goggler gang!" Frank shouted. "Come on, Joe!"

The boys ran back to their convertible, jumped in, and sped in pursuit. They could see the hardtop's taillights twinkling in the distance. Luckily the street was almost deserted.

"Radio the police!" Frank said, hunching over the wheel. Joe did so.

The hardtop shot through a red light ahead. Frank had to slam on the brakes as a car turned in front of him. Then he gunned after their quarry. Rounding a corner on screeching wheels, the getaway car sped eastward.

"He's heading for the Willow River bridge!" Joe exclaimed.

The river gleamed in the distance as the boys entered a wooded park section at the town's edge. Suddenly there was a deafening bang in front of them.

"A punctured tire!" Joe cried out.

The car ahead lurched and spun out of control, then careened into a ditch!

CHAPTER V

The River Spy

FRANK swung off the road and braked to a screeching halt. Both boys sprang out.

The blue hardtop was lying on its side, the wheels still spinning. Before the Hardys could reach it, the upper door swung open and the holdup man climbed free. But it was clear he was dazed or injured. He took a few staggering steps and toppled face forward.

The boys were at his side in a moment. The man moaned, then lifted his head painfully. The faint moonlight revealed a swarthy, hook-nosed face. Apparently he had jerked off his spectacles and stocking mask while driving.

"Are you hurt?" Frank asked.

"I . . . I don't know." Wincing, the man struggled to push himself upright.

Frank hastily frisked him. "Grab his arm, Joe, and help me swing him over so I can search his other coat pocket."

The boys noticed that the man was wearing gloves. As they maneuvered him into a sitting position, he screeched in agony. "Ow! . . . My knee!"

"Sorry," Joe murmured.

The boys propped the stranger as comfortably as they could against a nearby tree. Frank felt in his other pocket and found no weapon. Noticing the youths' calm, expert manner, the holdup man snarled, "Who are you punks, anyhow?"

"Frank and Joe Hardy, if that makes any difference," Frank replied evenly. "Our dad's a private investigator."

The man's eyes gleamed as if in recognition.

"I'll watch him, Joe. Go give the police another call."

"Right!"

But as Joe turned away, the man plucked at his trouser leg. "No! Wait!" the thief exclaimed desperately. "I'll make a deal with you! This job didn't amount to much—the cash box is in the wreck somewhere. But if you guys let me go, I'll put you onto something big—really big! I'll tell you who copped the Jeweled Siva!"

"The Jeweled Siva?" Joe paused in surprise.

"We'll listen, but we're making no deals," Frank said. As the holdup man glared at them, Frank jerked his head toward the convertible. "Go ahead and make that call, Joe."

His brother strode back to their car. The thief was groaning and clutching his knee. Frank glanced up the road to see if any other cars were approaching.

Without warning, one of his feet was yanked off the ground! Frank landed heavily on his back. "Joe! Help!" he yelled.

The thief sprang up and raced toward the bridge.

"Stop him!" Frank scrambled to his feet and both boys sprinted after the fleeing holdup man.

But the fugitive reached the bridge far ahead of them. In one swift movement he hoisted himself to the steel railing and dived headfirst into the water.

The Hardys reached the spot moments later. By now, the moon had clouded over again and the river was shrouded in darkness. Nothing could be heard except the lapping of the water against the bridge piers. The boys were furious at themselves.

"We would have to fall for that hurt knee gag!" Joe stormed.

"I sure *fell*," Frank said in disgust.

The police soon arrived and a search was made along both banks, but without success. Then the boys went to headquarters to check over the mug shots, but the thief's picture was not among them. By the time Frank and Joe got back to the Bijou,

"Joe! Help!" Frank yelled

the show was long over. Eventually they found Iola and Callie with Chet at the Hot Rocket.

"Well! At last!" Iola, a slender, dark-haired girl, greeted the Hardys with an eager smile. "Instinct tells me you two got involved in that movie holdup!"

"How'd you guess?" asked Joe.

Chet groaned. "I knew it! Send these two on a perfectly innocent errand and they get mixed up with a gang of crooks!"

"Not a gang." Frank smiled. "Just one—and he got away."

"Sounds exciting! Tell us about it!" begged Callie, a pretty brown-eyed blonde.

The Hardys related what had happened and apologized for leaving the two girls stranded. "You're excused." Iola giggled. "It didn't take us long to locate my brother!"

"Listen, I should be in bed by now, getting my rest," Chet complained.

"Okay," Joe said. "But at least give us time for a hamburger if we're going to foot the bill."

When the brothers reached home, their mother and Aunt Gertrude had already retired for the night. But Fenton Hardy was going over some case reports in his study. Frank and Joe told him of their exciting adventures.

"You boys have had a full night," Mr. Hardy commented. He rubbed his jaw thoughtfully and added, "It's odd that a member of the Goggler gang should rob a small movie theater."

"How come, Dad?" Frank asked.

"That gang has pulled some of the biggest jobs in this part of the country—bank stickups and jewel thefts. A petty crime like this is something new for them."

"Do you suppose that deal he offered us was on the level—to tell us who stole the Jeweled Siva?" Joe put in.

"Hard to say," the investigator replied. "It almost sounds as if he'd broken with the gang and was out for vengeance. Incidentally, I've been asked to take on that Jeweled Siva case."

The boys were elated. But their father told them he would be unable to handle the case until he found the swindler, Ace Pampton, whom he had been engaged to track down.

"Pampton's trail led here to Bayport," Mr. Hardy went on, "but I found out this evening he hopped a plane for St. Louis, so I'm going there myself on the first flight tomorrow morning. Suppose you boys go to see the owner of the Jeweled Siva and get all the preliminary facts."

"Do you mean it, Dad?" Joe said eagerly.

"Certainly. That would be a real help. The owner's an elderly woman named Mrs. Lunberry. She lives at a little place called Brockton up Willow River."

"Great! We'll go there on the *Sleuth* first thing tomorrow," Frank promised.

By eight o'clock the next morning the Hardy boys were steering their motorboat out of Barmet Bay into the mouth of the river. As they neared the bridge, the brothers saw a tow truck hoisting the movie thief's getaway car out of the ditch.

"Let's see if there's any news of the holdup man," Frank proposed.

Joe swerved toward shore and they moored the boat to the bridge abutment. A police detective named Reilly was supervising the hoisting operation.

"Find any clues?" Frank asked.

Reilly shook his head. "The cash box was in the car with the money spilled out, but I guess you fellows know that. No fingerprints."

"We noticed the thief wore gloves," Joe remarked.

"His gun must've been lying on the seat—it fell out the window when he tipped over," the detective added. "It was under the car."

"Lucky break for us, I guess," Frank said. "Have you traced the car yet?"

"It was stolen from a new-car storage lot. The company is Izmir Motors over in Ocean City." Reilly gestured toward the tow truck which bore the name of the same firm. "The license plates were stolen too."

The car was a brand-new Torpedo V-8.

"Too bad it had to get banged up that way," Joe said, admiring its sleek lines.

As the *Sleuth* proceeded upriver, Frank noticed a shiny green sedan parked on the road overlooking the shore. Farther on, he saw it cruising along slowly. As their boat passed a grove of trees, he was surprised to find it parked again.

"That car must be tailing us!" he exclaimed.

As Joe gunned the *Sleuth* toward shore for a closer look, Frank snatched up binoculars. The car sped off and he had time to spot only the first part of the license number—DZ 7.

"That's odd," he muttered, lowering the glasses.

"What's odd?"

"Joe, it may be just a coincidence, but that job was a brand-new Torpedo V-8!"

CHAPTER VI

Oriental Curse

"DID you get a look at the driver?" Joe asked.

Frank shook his head ruefully. "I was trying to focus on the license, but got only part of it—DZ 7. I think there was a man at the wheel waiting, and another fellow jumped in."

Puzzled, the Hardys continued upriver. Forty minutes later they reached the little village of Brockton and tied up at the public boat landing. A little boy with a sunburned nose who was fishing off the dock with a bamboo pole scowled at them.

"Can you tell us where Mrs. Lunberry lives?" Frank asked him with a smile.

"That gray cottage over near the woods." The lad indicated the direction with a jerk of his head and kept on scowling. "You guys realize you just scared off a big fat bluegill?"

Joe grinned. "Sorry, pal. Next time we'll keep our big fat boat out of your way."

The Hardys strode to the cottage. Their knock was answered by a silver-haired, elderly woman, bent and careworn.

"We're Frank and Joe Hardy," Frank explained. "You called our father about the Jeweled Siva."

"Oh, yes! Come in, come in!" she replied. "Will Mr. Hardy be able to take the case?"

"Not yet. But he asked us to get the facts."

Mrs. Lunberry invited the boys to sit down. Frank and Joe glanced about the small living room. The furnishings were comfortable but meager. They noticed well-worn books, some antique-looking pottery, and framed photographs of people apparently in outdoor foreign scenes.

"I can imagine what you're thinking," said Mrs. Lunberry as she seated herself on the faded chintz-covered sofa. "You're wondering how someone as poor as I am ever happened to own such a priceless object as the Jeweled Siva. Well, there's a long story attached to it."

"We'd like to hear it," Joe murmured.

"My late husband, Clarence Lunberry, was an archaeologist," the woman began. "He went on expeditions all over the world, to dig among ancient ruins. Often I went with him."

"Did he bring the Jeweled Siva back from one of his expeditions?" Frank asked.

"Yes, from a remote jungly part of India called Tripura. He had heard of a lost temple there and after many hardships he found it. The temple had fallen into ruins, but a beautiful little jeweled carving of the god Siva was still inside. The natives told him a curse would fall on anyone who disturbed the figure, but Clarence ignored their warnings and got permission to take the idol with him."

"The curse didn't come true, I hope," said Joe.

Mrs. Lunberry shook her head sadly. "Indeed, it did. Two members of the expedition died—one from malaria and one from being mauled by a leopard. Clarence himself had all sorts of bad luck after that. He was crippled in an accident and had financial troubles, but he always refused to give up the Jeweled Siva."

The widow said that she had kept the figure after her husband's death. But with her funds almost gone, she had finally been forced to put it up for sale. The tiny idol had been on display in the shop of an art and antique dealer named Fontana in New York City.

"Won't Fontana's insurance company pay you for the loss of the figure?" Frank queried.

"Ordinarily the company would pay for such a theft, but not in this case," Mrs. Lunberry replied. "You see, when I arranged to let Mr. Fontana handle the sale of the Siva, a business contract was drawn up to cover our agreement.

But I know little about such things and I was slow in getting the papers signed."

"You mean, there was no contract in force when the Jeweled Siva was stolen?" Frank asked.

"Exactly. And the insurance company requires one on all items that Mr. Fontana takes into his store to sell for an outside owner. So, I shan't get a penny. I don't know what I'll do if your father or the police don't find the Siva!"

Mrs. Lunberry's voice broke and she dabbed her eyes with a handkerchief. "Oh, dear! I almost believe there *is* a curse on that figure!"

Frank and Joe did their best to comfort her.

"Dad will certainly do everything he can, Mrs. Lunberry," Frank promised. "And so will we."

Suddenly the woman's face went white. She sucked in her breath sharply, then gave a piercing scream!

"What's wrong?" Joe cried out. Both boys sprang up from their chairs.

"The window! I saw something!" she gasped hysterically. "Like a head with no face! It was horrible!" The elderly woman was trembling.

"We'll see who's out there!" Frank told her, and the boys dashed outside.

"There he goes!" Joe yelled, pointing as they rounded a corner of the cottage.

A man with a stocking mask over his head was running toward the woods! Frank and Joe sprinted in pursuit. They plunged in among the trees. At first they were guided by faint sounds of rustling shrubbery and steps trampling dry leaves. Then, as the Hardys groped and darted about in the forest gloom, the sounds faded. The boys were forced to slow down and search the crushed underbrush for signs of the fugitive's trail.

"It's hopeless," Frank groaned at last. "He could be a mile from here by now!"

Disgusted, the Hardys walked back to Mrs. Lunberry's cottage. Frank stopped short.

"Look there, Joe! Under the window!"

The crude drawing of an eye had been chalked on the gray clapboard siding! The oval pupil and spark lines were instantly recognizable.

"Just like the glass eye and the drawing on Zatta's card!" Joe said grimly.

When the brothers went back to the cottage, they found Mrs. Lunberry pale but much calmer. She offered the boys some tea.

"No, thanks," said Frank. "We'd like to show you something if you're feeling all right."

"Of course." Mrs. Lunberry sounded a bit apprehensive, but she accompanied the boys outside. The sinister drawing of the eye seemed to frighten her again.

"Ever seen anything like it before?" Joe asked.

"Yes, I'm almost certain I have," she said shakily. "Perhaps it was in connection with my husband's work, but—oh, dear, I just can't think right now. It may come back to me later."

Frank promised that their father would get in touch with her as soon as he was free to work on the case. He also asked Mrs. Lunberry to let them know if she recollected where she had seen such an eye.

"I'm sure it signifies something terrible!" she said uneasily. "It's probably connected with the curse on the Jeweled Siva!"

Frank and Joe said good-by and walked back to the boat landing. They hoped the fisherboy would be there. The mysterious man might have quizzed him. But the lad was gone. The Hardys got into the *Sleuth* and headed for Bayport.

"Do you suppose that guy in the stocking mask was the same one who trailed us in the green Torpedo car?" Joe mused.

"I don't know," Frank replied, "but let's check on that auto dealership in Ocean City."

When working on a case, the brothers usually kept the *Sleuth's* radio turned on to pick up any calls from home. Just as they neared the mouth of Barmet Bay, Tony Prito's voice came over the speaker:

"*Napoli* calling *Sleuth!* . . . Come in, please."

The *Napoli* was Tony's own speedy little craft.

"*Sleuth* at mouth of river," Frank replied, picking up the microphone. "What's happened, Tony?"

Their chum asked, "When will you be back?"

"We're on our way now. Why?"

"Somebody was asking for you. I'll tell you all about it when you get here," Tony replied. "Over and out."

"Hmm. Wonder what *that* was all about," Frank muttered as he put down the mike. Joe shrugged.

Rounding out of the river into the bay, the *Sleuth* bounded over the waves toward their boathouse. As they neared it, another motorboat put-putted out to meet them.

"It's the *Napoli!*" Joe remarked.

Tony drew alongside. "Chet Morton wants to see you two as soon as possible," he reported.

"He's the one who was asking for us?" Frank inquired.

"Right. Chet says it's urgent. He wants you to meet him at Doc Grafton's Health Farm at eleven-thirty."

Frank glanced at his wristwatch. "Only a quarter to eleven. What say we stop at the hospital first and see how Bill Braxton's making out?"

"Good idea," Joe agreed as he berthed the *Sleuth*.

The boys drove to Bayport General Hospital and went to Braxton's room.

"Hi, fellows!" he greeted them. The mechanic was lounging in a chair, reading a magazine.

Frank grinned. "You don't look very sick."

"Me? I'm rarin' to go. Luckily I have a very thick skull—from being a racing driver, I guess."

"No aftereffects from that clout on the noggin?" Joe asked.

"Not a bit. The doctor was afraid I might have suffered a concussion, so they kept me for observation. But they're discharging me today."

The boys discussed with Bill the mysterious attack on him. "So Lambert's a crook named Spotty Lemuel," Bill said. "Wonder why he picked on me!"

Frank asked, "How did Spotty first hear about your hydrofoil, by the way?"

Bill wrinkled his forehead. "Don't know exactly. I met him at the track once in Ocean City. I drive stock cars over there, you know—for Izmir Motors."

Izmir Motors! Frank and Joe looked startled at hearing the name of the auto dealership.

"Something wrong?" Bill asked, puzzled.

"We're not sure," Frank said. "But it happens we were planning to check on that same place."

Leaving the hospital, the Hardys drove out of town to the health resort. It was located on a hillside overlooking the bay. Its wooded rolling acres were enclosed by a high wire fence. Brass letters arching over the driveway proclaimed: DOC GRAFTON'S HEALTH FARM.

Chet was waiting at the entrance for the Hardys. His usually calm face looked excited.

"I just found out you guys are going to be kidnapped!" he said.

CHAPTER VII

Beach Battle

"Kidnapped?" Joe echoed. "Are you serious?"

"Of course I'm serious!" Chet retorted.

The chubby youth was wearing white trousers and a green gym shirt with the name of the health resort in white letters across his chest.

"Okay, tell us," Frank said.

Chet gave a worried glance behind him. "I can't talk about it here," he whispered. "I quit at noon. Wait and I'll tell you the whole story."

"If you're not going to tell us till twelve o'clock," Joe said, exasperated, "why'd you get us up here at eleven-thirty?"

" 'Cause you two are always chasing around on some goofy mystery case, that's why. I wanted to make sure you'd be here in plenty of time." Chet regarded the young sleuths somberly. "Boy, if this tip I got is right, you fellows have really got yourselves in a spot. I wouldn't want to be in *your* shoes!"

"Stop looking so smug," Frank said. "What are we supposed to do—park here and just worry?"

"Come on inside and I'll show you around," Chet invited. "Wait a second."

He hurried over to a small stone gatehouse and spoke to the uniformed gatekeeper. The man gave Frank and Joe a brief once-over and nodded. "Okay. Just this once."

The Hardys hopped from the convertible and the three boys started up the curving graveled drive.

"How come you get off so early?" Joe asked.

"Well, it's my first day," Chet replied, "so all they had me come in for was to learn my way around and get a uniform and stuff like that. Besides, I have an after-dinner athletic period tonight."

The emerald lawn swept upward to a large white porticoed building. On a stone-flagged terrace in front, guests were sunning themselves in deck chairs. Several outbuildings could be glimpsed, set back among tall oak trees.

"Some layout," Frank murmured admiringly.

"You bet! It's strictly for guys with big bankrolls," Chet boasted.

As the boys stood chatting and looking around, a burly man with a shock of thick black hair came toward them. He also wore a green gym shirt, revealing sloping, muscular shoulders and furry, apelike arms. His nose was flat and almost shapeless. Cauliflower ears stuck out of his bulletlike head.

"Good grief, who's he?" Joe muttered.

"The bouncer, probably," Frank said. "I'll bet he's coming to give us the heave-ho."

"Relax—he's harmless," Chet assured them." "His name's Rip Sinder. Used to box heavyweight when Doc Grafton was a fight manager and trainer. Now he's sort of a general handyman. Incidentally, don't be surprised at the noises Rip makes. He got punched in the Adam's apple and it damaged his vocal cords so he can't talk."

The ex-pug approached and handed Frank a note penciled in spidery handwriting. It read:

I'd like to talk to you about
Braxton's hydrofoil.

Z. Mudge

Frank looked surprised. "Where is Mr. Mudge?"

Rip Sinder gave a guttural grunt and made stabbing gestures toward the terrace.

"Thank you." Frank restrained a start as he took in the boxer's huge, sausage-fingered hands.

"Come on. Let's go see him," Joe said. He whispered to his brother, "What's wrong?"

"Did you get a look at Sinder's hands?"

"Big, aren't they?" Chet said.

"I'll say they're big," Frank retorted under his breath. "Just like the pair of hands that tried to throttle me last night!"

Chet shuddered. "You don't mean Rip did it?"

Frank shrugged. "Probably a coincidence. But I'd like to get *my* hands on the person—whoever he is."

The pudgy lad groaned. "Remind me to keep away from you two. You *attract* trouble!"

Zachary Mudge was seated in a deck chair with his spindly legs stretched out. As before, he was clad only in shorts and a straw hat.

"Did you want to see us, sir?" Frank said.

"What? Speak up, boy!" As Frank repeated his words in a bellow, Mr. Mudge fiddled with his hearing aid. "All right, all right! You don't have to shout—I'm not deaf. Certainly I want to see you. Why do you think I sent for you?"

"Well, here we are, sir," Joe said, grinning.

"What about that fellow Braxton? Is he out of the hospital yet?"

"He's getting out today, sir." Suddenly Joe snapped his fingers. "Frank! We forgot to tell Braxton about Mr. Mudge!"

The elderly man snorted contemptuously. "Typical! You young whippersnappers wouldn't remember to come in out of the rain if someone didn't remind you. How about Lambert? Has he made Braxton an offer yet?"

"No, sir. Braxton hasn't seen him," Frank replied.

Mudge cackled and rubbed his hands in glee.

"Fine! Then there's still time to sew things up! All right, sonnies." Settling back, Mudge pulled his straw hat down over his face.

"What a character!" Chet Morton whispered as the boys walked away.

Chet hurriedly showed Frank and Joe through the splendid gymnasium building. This included a pool, steam room, tiled showers, and handball courts. The main room was equipped with exercise mats, trampolines, pulley weights, and other apparatus. Chet dropped several broad hints about his prowess as a gymnast.

"Okay, let's see you perform on that," Joe challenged, pointing to a leather horse.

"Not now. I have to change." Seeing the Hardys' grins, Chet burst out, "Okay, if you think I can't! I'll show you!"

Seizing the steel grips, he hoisted himself off the floor, getting somewhat red in the face. Then he tried to swing his legs around the horse. But as he let go with one hand, his grip with the other loosened.

"Oops!" Frank cried, and Chet landed heavily on the mat in a sitting position.

"That doggone handgrip was slippery!" Chet explained, wincing as he got up.

"Sure." Joe repressed a smile. "Anyhow, it was a good try."

Chet changed clothes in the locker room and the three boys walked back down the drive.

"Well, it's noon and you're through here," Frank reminded Chet. "How soon do we get briefed on that kidnapping tip?"

Just then Chet's yellow jalopy drove up outside the gateway. Two girls sat in the front.

"Hey! Iola and Callie!" Joe exclaimed.

The girls waved gaily and the trio hurried to meet them. Chet was chuckling as he ran.

"Well, fellows, it's like this," he said. "You're about to be kidnapped by two dangerous dolls—for a beach party!"

Frank and Joe stopped short, their jaws dropping open in surprise. Chet, Iola, and Callie burst into peals of laughter.

"Man, did I ever have these guys going!" Chet informed his two conspirators. "They were expecting some big underworld trap!"

"Who's complaining?" Frank retorted with a grin. "Callie can kidnap me any day."

"They even brought our surfboards!" Joe said.

"And your trunks and *two* picnic hampers!" Chet added, peering into the back seat. "Let's go!"

Callie rode with Frank in the convertible, while Joe piled in with Iola and Chet. They drove to a spot just north of Barmet Bay, called Gremlin Beach, which had become popular for surf-riding because of its high swells.

"What a day for surf-birds!" Joe cried as the foursome jumped out onto the clean white stretch of sand. An onshore breeze was blowing, and the waves from some distant storm were piling into high-crested breakers. Two boats came into view, kicking up plumes of spray.

"Tony and Biff!" Frank exclaimed. Biff Hooper was another Bayport High pal.

The *Napoli* and Biff's boat, the *Envoy*, soon arrived. Both boys had brought dates. In a few minutes the young people were frolicking in the water. Frank and Joe, expert surf-riders, brought screams of delight from the girls. They soared and dipped like skimming sea gulls.

Biff tried and did a "wipe out," coming up from the spill with a mouthful of salt water.

Presently the girls went ashore to broil hamburgers and frankfurters. Joe, glancing shoreward, noticed a youth with sun-bleached hair talking to Iola. She looked annoyed. Suddenly Joe's pulse skipped a beat.

"Hey, Frank!" he called. "It's that wise guy who checked our 'pass' at the empty house last night!"

The Hardys bounded out of the water. The stranger saw them coming and beat a hasty retreat. But Joe grabbed his arm. "Hold it, Buster! You have some explaining to do!"

In answer the youth swung a surprise blow at Joe's jaw, knocking him off balance. But Frank darted after the attacker and tackled him.

"Now start talking!" Frank ordered, letting him get up.

The youth said his name was Fred Hare and

that he was spending a week at a resort hotel in Bayport with his parents. He told the Hardys he had been paid five dollars to act as lookout at the house on Malabar Road.

"By whom?"

"Some man I met on the street. I never saw him before," Fred Hare whined. His description of the man was vague.

"Could have been Spotty Lemuel," Joe said.

At a call from Tony, the Hardys turned their heads. Fred seized his chance and sprinted toward a sand dune. Frank and Joe took after him, but as they topped the dune they saw him leap into a boat.

"I fed you guys a pack of lies!" he jeered, and gunned the motor. "I know plenty more!" The boat sped off.

Joe was furious, but Frank calmly strode back to their convertible to call Chief Collig. As the radio warmed up, the Hardys were startled to hear Aunt Gertrude's voice over the speaker.

"Boys! Come home at once!" she said. "I've caught the scoundrel who's behind this mystery!"

CHAPTER VIII

$DZ7$——

"This is Frank, Aunt Gertrude! Who is the fellow you've caught?"

"I've no time to explain!" Miss Hardy's voice snapped back. "Just get home here at once and help me attend to him! Your mother is out. Over and out!"

The Hardy boys looked at each other in stunned surprise.

"Good night!" Joe gasped. "I wonder who it is she's nabbed."

"Your guess is as good as mine," Frank said. "Whoever it is, we'd better blast off in a hurry!".

Iola and Callie looked stricken when the Hardys announced they had to rush home. But Iola quickly recovered her impish good spirits. "Even detectives must eat!" She quickly handed hamburgers to Frank and Joe.

The Hardys ate quickly, then sped off along the

highway. Reaching town, they wove their way
through traffic to the house at Elm and High.

Frank and Joe dashed inside. The place seemed
strangely quiet.

"Aunt Gertrude! Where are you?" Joe yelled.

The boys hurried downstairs to the basement
where the Hardys' short-wave set was located. No
one was there.

"Something must have happened to her!"
Frank said fearfully.

They ran up from the basement, then mounted
the hall stairway two steps at a time. Faint noises
drew Frank to their father's study. He burst in
and stopped short with a gasp.

"She's in here, Joe!" he called.

Miss Hardy was bound to a chair. Her mouth
was covered with a man's handkerchief, but her
eyes flashed fire. A warning had been lettered on
a piece of paper and clipped to the collar of her
blouse:

TAKE MY ADVICE AND KEEP THIS
BLABBERMOUTH GAGGED ALL THE TIME!

Frank and Joe hastily untied their aunt.

"Well! It's about time you two got here!" she
fumed as the handkerchief was removed. "Thank
heavens you finally did!"

"What happened, Aunty?" Frank asked.

Miss Hardy was not ready to tell her story just
yet. Declaring that she felt faint, she sank into an

easy chair and called for smelling salts and a cup of strong tea. At last she began to tell what had happened.

"Your mother went downtown this afternoon," Aunt Gertrude began. "Then a bit later a meter reader from the lighting company knocked at the back door and went down into the basement. I was busy straightening up and didn't hear him go out. But I assumed he had left after a couple of minutes."

"Go on!" Joe urged.

"Would you believe it, I discovered him here in your father's study trying to crack open the safe!"

For the first time, the boys looked over at the steel safe.

"Leapin' lizards!" Joe cried.

Chalked on the door was the same drawing of an eye that Frank and Joe had found under Mrs. Lunberry's window!

The safe door seemed to be securely closed, but the metal showed deep gouge marks and a broken drill bit lay on the floor nearby amid fragments of metal and some pottery.

"Looks as though he never did manage to get into the safe," Frank remarked.

"Indeed he didn't!" Gertrude Hardy retorted. "I snatched up a vase from the hallway table and struck him over the head with it. The man was— out cold, I believe you two would say."

Frank's and Joe's faces broke into broad grins. "Nice work, Aunty," said Frank. "Is that when you went downstairs and called us over the radio?"

"Yes," Aunt Gertrude went on, "but when I came back up to check on him, the scoundrel had revived. This time he waved a small bottle of nitroglycerine that he'd brought to blast open the safe, and threatened to blow up the house. I—well —became faint with nervous shock and that was when he tied me up. But not before I gave him a good piece of my mind!"

The two boys darted a glance at each other. They admired Aunt Gertrude's spirit, and pictured her scolding the intruder roundly as long as she could. No wonder he had clipped on the blabbermouth sign!

"I guess he cleared out suspecting you'd called for help," said Frank. "What did he look like?"

Miss Hardy replied promptly, "The man was clearly a criminal type—I could tell that from the shape of his ears!"

Joe smiled. "And the fact that he was cracking a safe," he said innocently.

"Never mind the jokes, young man. Features do reveal character." Miss Hardy asked for pencil and paper and sketched the intruder's ears. She added, "He was about five feet eight, blond, broad-shouldered, and had a tooth missing in front."

"You're very observant, Aunt Gertrude," Frank

said sincerely. Turning to his brother, he remarked, "It sure wasn't Spotty Lemuel."

Joe agreed, suggesting the intruder might have been the masked man who had eavesdropped at Mrs. Lunberry's house. Suddenly Joe slapped his forehead. "Boy, we're really batting a thousand today! We never did call the chief about Fred Hare!"

"We'd better phone him right now." Frank made the call, giving Collig a complete rundown.

The brothers, although eager to resume their sleuthing, decided to stay at home for the day in case the safecracker returned.

The next morning after breakfast the Hardy boys drove to Ocean City and asked directions to Izmir Motors. The automobile dealership was located in a low, white, modernistic building with a glass-fronted showroom. At one side was the used-car display lot. Parked in an open field at the rear were row upon row of gleaming new Torpedo sedans, station wagons, and convertibles awaiting sale.

"This outfit must do a big business," Joe remarked.

The boys prowled around, peering at the license number of every green Torpedo sedan. Those on the new-car lot had no plates, but there was one on display among the used cars and another—evidently a salesman's demonstrator —standing near the building. Neither checked out.

Around the corner, however, they spotted a third green sedan parked at the curb.

Its license number was DZ 736–421!

"Wow! Maybe we've struck oil!" Joe exclaimed.

The boys hurried into the showroom and were greeted by a dapper-looking salesman.

"We'd like to speak to the manager," Frank said.

"Right over there in the office."

The manager, a balding and middle-aged man with rimless glasses, was speaking on the telephone. A desk name plate identified him as H. J. Sykes, Sales Manager. As he finished talking, he gave the Hardys a cold, narrow-eyed stare. Finally he hung up. "Something I can do for you?"

Frank then began, "We're trying to trace a car, sir."

"What for?" Sykes broke in curtly.

"Our father, Fenton Hardy, is a private investigator—it's in connection with one of his cases," Frank explained. "I think the car we're after is parked right around the corner. It's a new green Torpedo sedan, license number DZ 736–421. Can you tell us who owns it, please?"

"No, I can't!" the manager snapped. "My time's valuable. I have other things to do than to help amateur private eyes."

His rudeness stung Joe into retorting, "Maybe you'd rather have us go to the police!"

"The police?" Sykes cleared his throat uncomfortably and finally stood up. "Oh, very well. Wait here. I'll check our files."

He strode to an adjoining office and returned a few minutes later. "Sorry, I can't help you. None of our personnel owns the car."

Frank and Joe exchanged glances and Frank said, "Thanks for your trouble."

They walked out of the showroom, feeling Sykes' eyes on their backs.

"Think he was keeping something back?" Joe muttered.

"I'd bet on it," Frank said. "Let's go take another look at that car."

They rounded the corner and stopped short. *The green sedan was gone!*

"That creep tricked us!" Joe blurted angrily. "I'll bet he had someone drive it away while he was pretending to check license numbers!"

Frank scowled. "Maybe the car will come back, once they think we're gone. Let's stake out the place and see what happens."

"Good idea!"

The boys drove off, past the showroom. Frank kept going until they were sure no one was tailing them. Then he circled around and parked on a side street near Izmir Motors.

"I noticed a diner right near where the green sedan was standing," Frank said to Joe. "How about you going in there and keeping watch? I'll

take that drugstore right across from the showroom."

"Roger!"

The morning dragged by. The boys met each
other from time to time to exchange reports, and
switched positions occasionally. All day long they
kept up their dogged watch. The showroom remained open in the evening.

At last their vigilance paid off. Shortly before
nine o'clock both boys noticed the green sedan
they were watching for cruise slowly around the
block. In the dusk it was difficult to make out the
driver's face.

Frank and Joe hastily got their convertible. As
they drove back toward the showroom, they saw
the green sedan suddenly speed away.

"He must have spotted us!" Joe exclaimed.

Frank gunned in pursuit and kept the car in
view. The driver wove his way through the mid-
town traffic. Near the outskirts of Ocean City, the
Torpedo increased speed and lengthened the distance between the two cars. Frank and Joe saw by
its taillights that it had turned up a side road.

By this time, darkness had fallen. Frank had
switched off their headlights as they left the traf-
ficked streets behind, so as not to be seen in the
sedan's rear-view mirror.

The turnoff taken by the Torpedo was an un-
paved road, with only a few widely separated

street lights. One side of the road was wooded. On the other could be glimpsed the skeleton frames of several new houses under construction.

"Where'd he go?" Joe said, straining his eyes in the darkness. "Has he given us the slip?"

Frank toed the accelerator. "May as well turn on the lights," he muttered.

As the yellow head beams illumined the road, both boys gasped. Just ahead was an open excavation!

"Look out!" Joe yelled.

Frank tried to brake and swerve but there was no time. The convertible plunged downward, its front wheels landing with a jolt as the body banged against the frame! Shaken, the Hardys climbed out onto the road.

Frank groaned. "What a mess! It'll take a tow truck to—"

Both boys whirled suddenly at the sound of rushing footsteps. Two stocking-masked figures had darted from behind the trees fringing the road! Up-raised arms swung hard, and Frank and Joe sank to the ground, unconscious!

CHAPTER IX

A Cruise in the Sea Spook

WHEN Joe opened his eyes he found himself looking up at the night sky. It took him a moment to collect his wits. Then he realized he was lying in the road and struggled upright.

"Sufferin' snakes!" he muttered to himself. "How long have I been out? . . . Oooh!" His head throbbed from the blow he had received.

A faint moan nearby drew his attention.

"Frank!" Joe sprang to his feet and hurried to his brother's assistance. "Are you okay?"

"Sure, I—I guess so. . . . Whew! I'm still seeing stars, though."

Joe gave Frank a hand while he got up. Ruefully the brothers took stock of their position. Their car was nose down in the huge pothole.

"Boy, are we ever a couple of bird brains!" Frank said in disgust. "Take a look."

He pointed to several overturned wooden bar-
riers beside the road. Evidently they had been
used to block off the excavation. Nearby lay lan-
terns and warning flares—all extinguished.

"The whole setup was arranged beforehand—
and that green sedan led us right into the trap,"
Joe said.

"Which means someone must have spotted us
during the day when we were staked out at Izmir
Motors," Frank speculated.

"Right. And it could have been Sykes himself."

The Torpedo sedan, the boys reasoned, had
pulled off the road and among the trees before
reaching the excavation. Then the thugs had
waited for the Hardy's car to appear, hoping it
would plunge into the hole.

"What do you suppose they were after?" Joe
asked his brother.

"I can guess," Frank said. "The glass eye."

"Lucky we left it home."

Frank tried their convertible's two-way radio
and found it undamaged. He contacted the Ocean
City police operator. A prowl car arrived, followed
soon after by a tow truck from an all-night garage.
The convertible was hauled out of the excavation
and examined. Its front wheels had been jarred out
of alignment and the frame needed straightening,
so the Hardys had to return to Bayport by bus.

It was after midnight when they walked into
their house. Mrs. Hardy and Aunt Gertrude had

already gone to bed. Frank found a note in his mother's handwriting on the telephone pad.

"Hey, look at this, Joe!"

It said: *Bill Braxton tried to reach you twice this evening.*

"Wonder what's up," Joe said.

"It's probably too late to get him now. We'll have to wait until morning."

Next day, before breakfast, Frank called Braxton's boathouse.

"Boy, I'm glad you called early!" Bill said. "How'd you two like to take a cruise to Long Point with me on the *Sea Spook*?"

"Sounds terrific!" Frank said. Then he asked, "By the way, Bill, have you heard from a man named Zachary Mudge?"

"I sure did, and he told me he'd talked to you fellows. That's what this cruise is all about."

Braxton explained that Mr. Mudge was interested in forming a partnership to put the young mechanic's hydrofoil design into production. The craft would be built by one of Mudge's present companies—the Neptune Boatworks at Long Point. First, however, he wanted Braxton to take the boat there to be looked over and tried out by Neptune's chief engineer.

"There's to be a conference at one o'clock and a trial run at three—so we ought to shove off pronto. I'd like to get there by noon and have time to grab some lunch." Braxton added,

"There's a swell beach at Long Point. You two could have a swim while I'm at the boatworks."

An idea popped into Frank's mind. "Swell, Bill —count us in!"

Frank hurried to the table, where he and Joe excitedly discussed the cruise over breakfast. "Look!" Frank proposed. "We could hop a train at Long Point and be in New York City in less than an hour. That would give us a chance to talk to that art dealer about the Jeweled Siva and still get back in time for the trial run."

"Keen idea!" Joe agreed.

Mrs. Hardy had no objection to the trip, but Aunt Gertrude expressed grave doubts about the seaworthiness of Braxton's "contraption." "And what's all this about the Jeweled Siva?" she inquired, giving the boys a piercing stare.

"The Jeweled Siva is a valuable little idol from India. It was stolen," Frank explained. "Dad's going to take the case and we're doing some preliminary legwork for him."

"The idol has a curse on it, Aunt Gertrude!" Joe said. He proceeded to give her a blood-chilling version of the story the boys had heard from Mrs. Lunberry.

"Humph," said Miss Hardy. "If you think I believe one word of that nonsense about a curse, you're mistaken." But the boys could tell she was disturbed when she almost poured maple syrup into her coffee.

"What Joe told you is true, Aunty," Frank said, straight-faced but with a twinkle. "When we were at Mrs. Lunberry's a faceless figure peered in the window."

Mrs. Hardy became worried and begged the boys not to have anything more to do with the case. After much wheedling and reassurance, however, she was persuaded that they should continue.

"Whew!" Joe breathed as the boys started off for the boathouse. "Next time I start teasing Aunt Gertrude with any chills-and-thrills stuff remind me to keep my big mouth shut!"

"Ditto!" Frank said, grinning.

The *Sea Spook* was fueled and checked by the time they reached the bay. Soon it was scudding out of the harbor—rising on its hydrofoils as it picked up speed.

"Is the deal with Mr. Mudge all set?" Joe asked the *Spook's* skipper.

"Well, not quite. The slide-rule boys at the boatworks are going to look over my blueprints with a fine-tooth comb. Then the chief engineer will probably give this job a real workout on Long Point Sound." Braxton added with a confident smile, "But I think I can convince him."

The sun beat down hotly out of a cloudless sky and the Atlantic was running in calm swells as the *Sea Spook* tooled along the coast at thirty knots. Frank and Joe enjoyed the cruise immensely.

It was not yet noon when the craft docked at

Long Point. The Hardys hurried off to catch their train. By ten minutes to one it was pulling into New York City. They taxied through skyscrapered canyons to Fontana's art shop in Lower Manhattan. A sign in the window said:

OBJETS D'ART
Federico Fontana

Inside, the store was filled with paintings, pieces of sculpture, and tapestries. A clerk directed the boys to Mr. Fontana, a tall, distinguished-looking man with graying dark hair and beard.

"Of course I have heard of the famous detective, Fenton Hardy!" he said, shaking hands with Frank and Joe. "And I am most happy to hear that he will be taking the case."

"Will you tell us about the theft, please?" Frank asked.

Fontana related that the shop's burglar alarm had been cunningly disconnected by the thief or thieves, who had jimmied the back door.

Joe remarked, "Whoever did it must have cased this place pretty thoroughly beforehand."

"Exactly. No doubt he was one of the many people who came into my salon to browse around during the past few weeks."

"But you didn't notice anyone who struck you as suspicious?" Frank asked.

Fontana frowned and stroked his beard. "I recall one dark-skinned man. He wore a turban and appeared to be an East Indian. He asked many questions and fingered the Siva as if he hated to put it down. But unfortunately"—Fontana threw out his hands in despair—"I have no idea who he was."

"Nothing was taken except the Siva?"

"Nothing at all. A policeman passing by on his beat thought he saw a glimmer of light in the shop and tried the door. He went inside, but found the place dark and empty."

"Do you think the thieves could sell the Siva anywhere?" Joe asked.

"Definitely," Fontana replied. "There are many collectors who would buy such an exquisite object with no questions asked. The gems alone would bring ten thousand dollars."

Frank suddenly took out the glass eye. "Have you ever seen anything like this, sir?"

"But how intriguing!" The art dealer examined the eye with keen interest. "No, I have never seen such an object before. It is a most beautiful piece of craftsmanship—like the fine quality of Murano glass. Would you care to sell it?"

"I'm afraid not," Frank replied. "Have you any idea where it may have been made?"

Fontana shrugged, but suggested that it might have come from Venice, Italy. He asked the boys where they had obtained it. Frank said merely that they had found it and politely evaded any further questions. He and Joe thanked the art dealer and prepared to leave the shop.

As Joe was opening the door, he stopped short with a gasp. "Frank! Look!" he hissed.

A blind man with dark glasses and a tray of pencils was standing just across the street!

"That's Zatta, all right!" Frank exclaimed. "Let's go talk to him!"

The boys waited for a break in traffic and darted across. The blind man hastily walked away, tapping with his white cane. Joe plucked his sleeve.

"Get away from me!" Zatta snarled under his breath. "Go on! Beat it! . . . I'll get in touch with you later!"

Joe looked at his brother. Frank gave a puzzled shrug and the two boys dropped back among the other pedestrians. Frank flagged a taxi and told the driver, "Penn Station."

On the way, they continued to puzzle over the blind man's reaction. "Zatta sounded scared to death," Joe remarked. "I wonder if he was on the level about getting in touch with us."

"We'll just have to wait and see," Frank replied. "Maybe he's afraid of having talked too much already."

The brothers arrived at Long Point in plenty of time for the trial run. Bill Braxton, Frank, Joe, and the engineer Kurt Rummel started off in the *Sea Spook* on the dot of three. Boaters gaped as the hydrofoil streaked across the Sound.

Rummel seemed much impressed. "If she can

perform anything like this in heavy weather, you really have something here, Braxton!" he said.

Bill put the craft through a series of tight maneuvers. Plumes of spray flew in the air as the *Spook* pirouetted about gracefully. Suddenly she refused to come out of a turn.

"What's wrong?" Rummel asked with a frown.

"I don't know," Braxton muttered anxiously. "The rudder must be jammed!"

He dashed out of the cabin toward the fantail. Frank went aft with him to help. Braxton bent over the rail to peer down at the rudder linkage. At that instant the craft lurched and swung sharply to port! As it heeled over, Frank and Braxton were hurled into the water!

Terror chilled Joe. His brother and Bill Braxton might be mangled by the propeller or the foils!

CHAPTER X

Dangerous Dobermans

THE *Sea Spook* was spinning around Frank and Bill Braxton in a tight circle—completely out of control!

"Stop the engine!" Joe yelled to Rummel, and made his way out onto the tilting afterdeck.

The engineer flung an angry retort over his shoulder. He had already closed the throttle and was probing at the steering controls, hoping to get some response to the helm.

Joe could see the two figures floundering in the water. Flying spray from the *Spook* was blinding and half-drowning them. Joe was slipping and teetering on the wet deck, but he managed to unhook a life ring from the rail and toss it into the water.

The craft had so much way on from the high speed that it took the *Spook* some time to slow. Gradually her hull settled into the water. In a few moments the *Spook* came to a dead stop.

Frank and Bill Braxton, apparently unhurt, stroked their way over to the hydrofoil, blinking water out of their eyes. Joe and Rummel hauled them aboard.

"What went wrong, Bill?" Frank asked as they dried off with towels from the storage locker.

The young mechanic shook his head gloomily. "I don't know yet, except that the steering system failed. The rudder must have broken and slapped over to one side."

Kurt Rummel refrained from making any comment, but his face showed professional disapproval. A harbor patrol launch had observed their difficulties and was speeding out to their aid.

"Give us a towline!" Bill called over.

The *Sea Spook* was towed to the dry dock of the Neptune Boatworks. Here, Bill and the engineer gave the craft a thorough inspection.

"Well, there's the answer," Bill said angrily. "A sheared rudder pintle. It doesn't look to me like an accident, either!"

Rummel looked skeptical. "Your hydrofoil design is new enough to be revolutionary, Braxton. Those high-speed turns may put more stress on the steering than you realize. I think this calls for a whole new study of your design."

A new pintle was installed and the *Sea Spook* started home to Barmet Bay. Braxton was downcast over the outcome of the test.

"You really think it was sabotage?" Joe asked.

"Sure. But I can't prove it," Braxton replied.

"When was it done?" Frank asked. "It was docked in plain sight during your conference at the boatworks, wasn't it? There probably were people gawking at it every minute of the time."

"The dirty work could have been done right in my own boathouse," Braxton said bitterly. "The pintle was probably sawed partway through, but it took a few hours of operation to break off."

"Any idea who might have done it?" Frank asked.

Braxton shook his head. "Not a clue—unless it was someone who doesn't want the *Sea Spook* to go into production."

Frank and Joe exchanged thoughtful glances. "A figure in hiding!" Joe declared, and Frank added, "Who must be found!"

Nevertheless, both boys were wondering if the sabotage might have been committed for a different purpose—to injure them! Had someone guessed—or overheard—that the Hardys would go along on the *Spook's* next cruise, and had this person tried to cause an accident at sea?

Frank and Joe arrived home in the evening and learned that Chief Collig had telephoned. Frank called back but was unable to reach him at headquarters until the next morning. The chief reported that he had had word from the Ocean City police on the green Torpedo sedan.

"That license number you gave was registered

in the name of Malcolm Izmir, the owner of Izmir Motors," Collig informed Frank. "But the car had already been reported stolen."

"When did that happen—the theft, I mean?"

"The police weren't sure. Izmir's butler reported the theft the same evening he found the car missing. But he said it hadn't been used for a couple of days, so it might have been taken from Izmir's garage a day or two earlier."

Frank was disappointed. This left the question still unanswered as to who had been driving the green sedan on Wednesday during their trip up-river to Mrs. Lunberry's.

"Another thing," Collig said. "We called the hotels and found that kid, Fred Hare. He's staying with his parents at the Summerfield."

"Does his story check out?" Frank asked.

"It seems to. That crack about knowing more than he told you was just bragging. His father promised to give him a good talking to."

Frank grinned and thanked the chief. When Frank discussed the news with Joe, however, neither was satisfied with the story that Izmir's car had been stolen.

"Somehow it sounds phony," Frank said. "Especially the butler's not being sure when the car was taken!"

"It strikes me the same way," Frank agreed. "I vote we do some more checking when we go to Ocean City to get our car."

Frank called the repair garage and was told that their convertible was ready for pickup. Meanwhile, Joe had had a sudden idea.

"We've been passing up an easy lead on this case!" he exclaimed.

"What's that?" Frank queried.

"Checking the calls Lambert made from his motel. The manager said all calls passed through the central switchboard, remember?"

Joe promptly leafed through the telephone directory and dialed the number of the Bayview Motel. His hunch paid off.

"Sure, we keep a record of all *outgoing* phone calls," the manager said. "The time and the number go right on the guest's bill after the desk clerk gets his party for him."

"Will you please look up and see if Lambert placed any calls while he was staying there?"

"Easy. Hold the phone." There was silence, then the manager's voice returned to the line. "Well, according to his bill, he made three calls—all to the same number."

Joe copied it down, thanked the motel manager, and hung up.

"That looks like an Ocean City listing," Frank remarked as he read the number. "Hmm. I wonder . . ."

Frank dialed Information and asked for the number of Izmir Motors in Ocean City. *It checked with the number on the pad!*

"Now we're getting some place!" Joe exclaimed. "Let's hop over to Ocean City right away!"

The boys caught a bus which dropped them not far from the repair garage. They got their car and drove to Izmir Motors.

This time, the Hardys walked straight through the showroom to Sykes' office. His face seemed to turn a shade paler as he caught sight of the brothers. He gave them a smile, took off his glasses, and began polishing them nervously.

"Come in, boys! . . . Please sit down."

Frank and Joe were struck by his change in manner.

"I suppose you've heard what happened to us the other night," Frank said coolly.

"Why, yes—yes, I did. The police informed me. A terrible thing! It upset me very much."

"Why didn't you tell us that was your boss's car when we gave you the license number?" Joe demanded.

Sykes looked embarrassed. "Believe me, I didn't know. Our office only keeps a record of the licenses of salesmen's cars and demonstrators—and Mr. Izmir wasn't here at the time."

"You sure weren't very cooperative."

"To tell the truth, I'd had a call about you two fellows," Sykes said sheepishly.

"What sort of a call?" Frank asked.

"An anonymous phone tip the previous afternoon—Wednesday, that is. It was a man's voice.

He warned me that two young fellows might drop in, trying to trace a license number. He said you were really a pair of gyps—shakedown artists. You were just setting things up to make a fake accident claim against a car owned by someone connected with Izmir Motors."

Joe gave the sales manager a scornful look. "You didn't even try to get his name?"

Sykes shrugged. "He hung up before I could ask. But I was still on my guard when you two walked in. Naturally I wasn't going to go out of my way to help you."

"Well, maybe you can help us now," Frank said. "Have you ever heard of a man named Lambert— or Spotty Lemuel?"

The sales manager shook his head. "No, I don't believe so."

"Here's a picture of him." Frank held out a photograph, borrowed from Mr. Hardy's files.

Sykes looked at it and again shook his head. "Never saw him in my life. Why?"

"Because he's mixed up in the case we're working on," Frank said, "and we have proof that he called Izmir Motors three times recently."

Sykes seemed startled and offered to check the firm's file of customers and prospects. But he soon came back and reported that his clerks could find no record of either name.

"We'd better speak to Mr. Izmir," Frank said.

The savage guard dogs raced toward them!

Sykes gulped. "Uh—I'm afraid that's impossible. He's not here."

Joe started to ask where they could get in touch with him, but Frank quickly interrupted and said they would call back later. When they got outside, Frank explained, "I figured it might be better if Sykes didn't know our next move. He might tip off Izmir we're coming."

"Quick thinking," Joe approved. "Maybe we can catch the boss man when he's not expecting us."

The boys checked Malcolm Izmir's name in a phone directory and drove to his home address. This proved to be a palatial walled estate in the hills overlooking Ocean City. Joe jabbed the gate bell repeatedly, but no one answered.

"You game to go over the top?" he asked Frank.

Frank sized up the situation warily. "Okay. At least we can find out if he's home."

The boys shinned directly over the gate.

"Good thing we didn't try climbing the wall," Joe muttered, pointing to a *cheval-de-frise* of broken glass strewn along the top.

Dropping down inside, they walked toward the house, which could be glimpsed beyond the trees. Suddenly the Hardys were chilled by ferocious snarls. They whirled, then froze in terror. Four sleek, fierce-eyed Doberman pinscher guard dogs were racing toward them!

"They're killers!" Frank cried out.

CHAPTER XI

A Midnight Deal

THE Hardys looked around wildly. There was no chance of getting back to the gate—the dogs were already cutting off their line of escape.

"That tree!" Frank yelled, pointing to a nearby copper beech with low-hanging branches.

The boys sprinted madly. Each grabbed a limb and swung himself off the ground.

The Dobermans came on like demons. Although lean and long-legged, they were powerful, deep-chested brutes. The dogs hurled themselves at the lower branches, baying and straining every muscle to reach their prey.

"Sufferin' catfish!" Joe quaked. "Those babies mean business!"

"If we fell out of this tree," Frank agreed uneasily, "we'd be hamburger in two minutes!"

"Just don't let go, that's all," Joe advised.

"Great. But what do we do for food and water?"

Both boys were perspiring as they stared around for signs of help.

"Ah! Thank goodness! Here comes someone!" Joe said.

A man—evidently a servant, wearing a house-boy's white jacket—was striding toward them. He was carrying a braided whip which Frank and Joe assumed was to use on the dogs in case they got out of hand.

"Heel!" he called sharply.

The Dobermans stopped barking and slunk close to his side. Then he glared up at the boys.

"What're you two doing up that tree?"

"Boy, there's a foolish question if I ever heard one!" Joe muttered. Out loud he retorted, "What does it look like?"

"Get down out of there and beat it before I call the cops!" the houseman ordered.

"Wait a minute—we're not burglars," Frank said. "We rang the bell at the gate but no one answered, so we had to climb over. We came here to see Mr. Izmir—on important business."

The servant studied the boys suspiciously. "That's out of the question," he said. "Mr. Izmir can see no one. He has suffered a nervous break-down. He's living in complete seclusion under a doctor's care."

Frank thought fast. "What we have to see Mr. Izmir about is *very* important," he said. "It has to do with a glass eye."

The servant's eyes widened and his jaw dropped open. He wet his lips slowly, then said in a more respectful voice, "Your names, please?"

"Frank and Joe Hardy."

"I'll inquire inside. Wait right there."

He turned and walked toward the house, leaving the dogs behind. The four Dobermans sat watching the boys in eager silence, tongues lolling.

"Wait right here, he says," Joe echoed resentfully. "What does he think we're going to do—climb down and play tag again with those four-legged meat grinders?"

In a few minutes the servant returned. "Mr. Izmir will see you," he announced. Turning to the dogs, he said simply, "Guard!"

Frank and Joe climbed down warily, keeping an eye on the Dobermans. The servant accompanied the boys to the house and led them inside to a richly furnished drawing room. There was a white, thick-piled carpet on the floor and modernistic paintings on the walls.

A man who was pacing back and forth restlessly turned abruptly to face the boys. He was of medium height, with a thick neck and bulging froglike eyes.

"Mr. Izmir?"

"Yes." He gave them each a quick handshake and waved them to a sofa. "Sit down, boys!"

Frank and Joe obeyed while mentally sizing up

their host. They both thought Malcolm Izmir looked healthy enough, although he seemed rather tense and jumpy.

"I understand you fellows want to see me about a—a glass eye?"

"That's right, sir," Frank said. "Also about a man named Lambert—or Lemuel."

Izmir's hooded eyes blinked. "Lambert? Lemuel? . . . Who's he? Does he have something to do with this—er—glass eye?"

"We're not sure. We think the eye may belong to him." Frank told briefly how he and Joe had found the eye aboard the *Sea Spook* and what had happened later when they tried to trace Lambert through the Bayview Motel.

"That's interesting. Very interesting," the auto dealer commented. "But what makes you think I might know anything about this fellow?"

"We know he called Izmir Motors from his motel three times," Joe said. "But your sales manager knows nothing about him and says he's not a customer or a prospect."

"Strange." Izmir frowned. "I can't imagine what his business with us would be—unless he knows someone who works for me. I'll have Sykes check into it. Do you have this glass eye with you?"

Frank shook his head. "No, sir. We left it back home for safekeeping. You see, the thieves who stole your car waylaid us the other night—and we think they were after the eye."

The Hardys watched Izmir's reaction closely. Again his reptilian eyes blinked. He seemed disappointed. "Too bad," he muttered. "I was hoping it might give us a clue—in fact, I had hoped you boys might even be able to help *me*."

Frank and Joe looked at each other.

"How do you mean, sir?" Frank asked.

"No doubt you were wondering about my watchdogs," Izmir replied, "and the fact that no one answered your ring at the gate. Well, it's because I've been receiving threats lately."

"What sort of threats?" Joe asked.

"Messages threatening my life. They come unsigned—except for a drawing of a horrible-looking eye." Izmir licked his lips. "That's why I agreed to see you at once when I heard you'd mentioned a glass eye. I thought there might be some connection."

The Hardys were startled.

"Our dad's a private detective," Frank said. "He's going to look into all this as soon as he winds up another case. We'll certainly let you know if we find out anything, Mr. Izmir."

The auto dealer nodded. "I appreciate that. But I won't be here after tomorrow."

"You're going away?" Joe asked.

"Yes, on a long cruise." Izmir stood up and began pacing about restlessly. "These threats have left my nerves all shot. I can't eat or sleep. So my doctor has advised a complete rest and change of scene. I'm sailing from New York Monday on the ocean liner *Cristobal*."

The Hardys thanked him for his time, and the houseman escorted them back to the gate.

"What do you make of Malcolm Izmir?" Joe asked his brother as they drove away.

"He must be scared of *something,* all right," Frank mused, "or else he wouldn't be holed up with those dogs guarding the place. Also, how did that car thief get past them? Anyhow, I'd like to know more about Izmir. Maybe Chief Collig can help us."

As soon as they reached Bayport, the boys drove to police headquarters. They told the chief what had happened at Ocean City and asked him if he knew Malcolm Izmir.

"I've heard of him," Collig replied. "He's one of the biggest businessmen in Ocean City—and quite a community leader. Has all sorts of projects. Izmir Motors is just one."

Joe shot his brother a puzzled glance. "He doesn't sound like the kind of person who would be mixed up in anything crooked."

Collig chuckled. "Not likely. I'll check on him, though, with Ocean City police."

Frank and Joe had a postponed picnic supper with Iola and Callie and it was close to midnight when they reached home. The hall telephone was ringing. Frank answered it as Joe waited.

"You're one of the Hardys?" a muffled voice asked.

"Yes—Frank Hardy. Who's speaking, please?"

"Never mind that. You know a peddler named Zatta? He's a stoolie for your father."

Frank was instantly alert. He signaled Joe to listen in. "What about Zatta?"

"I'm offering you Hardys a chance to save his life—*if* you promise not to call in the cops."

"What do you mean 'save his life'?" Frank said.

There was moment's silence. Then another voice, which Frank recognized as the one-eyed peddler's, came on the line.

"These guys are holding me prisoner!" Zatta croaked fearfully. "You've gotta help me! They'll kill me if you don't! Do what they ask you—please!"

Zatta's voice was choked off suddenly, as if he has been yanked away from the phone. The muffled voice returned. "Okay. You heard him. We're offering you his life for that glass eye."

Frank tried to stall for time, but the voice cut him short. "Yes or no? Is it a deal?"

"What are the terms?" Frank asked.

The voice instructed the Hardys to drive to a certain spot atop Lookout Hill, leave their car, and walk down to a meeting spot on the open hillside. The transfer would then be arranged.

Frank looked at his brother. Joe nodded. "Okay, we accept," Frank said.

"Remember—no double cross! You bring in the cops and Zatta's a dead pigeon! Be there in fifteen minutes—after that, it'll be too late."

Mrs. Hardy and Aunt Gertrude had awakened and asked what the message was. After a family conference it was decided that the boys would call Sam Radley, a trusted operative of their father's. He agreed to approach the hillside cautiously from the opposite direction and be ready to cover them in case of trouble.

Frank went upstairs for the glass eye, then the brothers hurried outside to their convertible and drove to Lookout Hill. They parked at the appointed spot near a narrow turnoff which led steeply downward to Shore Road, bordering Barmet Bay.

Frank and Joe left the car and made their way cautiously through a screen of trees. A dark figure on the hillside waved his arms. Hearts thumping, the Hardys walked toward him.

The figure had glowing eyes!

CHAPTER XII

Doom Ride!

As THE Hardys came close enough to make out the figure, they saw the reason for the glowing eyes. The man was wearing spectacles with bulging phosphorescent eyeballs. His head was shrouded in a stocking mask.

"Someone from the Goggler gang!" Joe hissed.

In the midnight silence the boys' footsteps crunched loudly in the grassy underbrush. Far below them, moonlight glinted on the waters of the bay.

"Okay. Stop right there!" the man ordered.

Frank and Joe obeyed. Both thought the masked man's voice sounded faintly familiar. They wondered if he might be Spotty Lemuel, but neither could be sure.

"Did you bring the glass eye?"

"We brought it," Frank said, "but we're not handing it over till we have Zatta."

The man turned and shone a flashlight down the hillside. He flicked the beam on and off twice.

The Hardys watched tensely. They saw an answering glow from Shore Road.

The masked man removed a pair of binoculars which were slung around his neck. He handed them to Frank and pointed toward the light. Frank raised the glasses to his eyes, then gasped.

"What is it?" Joe whispered.

"Zatta! They have him tied up down there at the foot of the drive!"

Frank passed the binoculars to Joe, who peered through them. The light on Shore Road was evidently coming from a bull's-eye lantern. It was aimed to illuminate the captive peddler. Zatta was lying bound and gagged.

"It looks as if he's unconscious!" Joe muttered. "His eyes are closed!"

"Don't worry—he's alive," the masked man said.

"He'd better be," Frank said. "You'll get the glass eye when we have him in the car and we're sure he's all right. Not before."

"And you two had better not try pulling any fast ones," the masked man retorted. "Wait right here till I get down the hill. Then drive your car there. You can load Zatta aboard and hand over the glass eye. After that, clear out and don't look back. Get me?"

Frank nodded. "Check."

The gangster strode off into the darkness, picking his way down the incline.

"I wonder if Sam got here," Joe whispered.

"I sure hope so," Frank replied. "Goggle Eyes could be pulling us right into a trap!" He added, "We'd better go through with it, though, for Zatta's sake. He must have stuck his neck out, giving Dad that tip."

Crickets chirped in the stillness. The eerie call of a night bird sounded somewhere overhead. Presently the light on Shore Road went out.

"That must be the signal," Frank murmured. "Let's go!"

The boys hurried back to their convertible and climbed in. The engine roared to life. Frank swung out from the curb, then turned right into the long, steep drive leading to Shore Road. Beyond was nothing but a gleam of water as the cliff sheered abruptly into the bay.

The car headlights revealed Zatta's motionless figure still lying across the foot of the drive. The masked man and whoever had come with him were nowhere in sight.

Joe glanced over at the grassy hillside. In the distance his eye caught a darting figure.

"Sam Radley!" Joe guessed.

Frank toed the brake pedal as he turned to look. The pedal caught for an instant—then sank to the floorboard without slowing the car!

Horrified, Frank pumped the pedal. *No response!* He yanked the hand brake and it gave easily without the slightest effect!

"Joe! Something's happened to our brakes!"

The convertible was gathering speed—hurtling straight down toward the helpless peddler!

"You'll go right over him!" Joe gasped.

"And off the cliff!"

The boys were paralyzed with fear. With no way to slow the car, it would be impossible to negotiate a turn onto Shore Road.

Frank shifted into low gear. The car bucked and lost a little speed. Noticing that the narrow drive was high-banked on either side, Frank swung right, scraping the convertible's side against the grassy slope.

Zatta lay less than fifty feet ahead!

As the bank flattened, Frank spun the wheel hard right. The car leaped from the drive onto the grass, bumping and jolting over the uneven ground. It shot across the corner of the hillside, slowing bit by bit. Then it slewed out across Shore Road.

Frank kept it parallel to the pavement, but suddenly there was a hard jolt as the left rear wheel went over the edge of the cliff. With a shudder, the convertible came to a dead halt—its body quivering on its springs!

The two boys sat still, white-faced and gasping. Then Frank slumped over the wheel.

"Whew!" he breathed. "I thought sure we'd had it!"

"We would have," Joe said, "if you hadn't downshifted and grazed that bank! Man, that was fast thinking!"

Frank shook his head dazedly. "I wouldn't even have known the brakes were gone if you hadn't called out about Sam!"

A streak of light shot up from the hillside, exploding into a starburst of red fire!

"It's Sam firing a Very pistol!" Joe cried out.

Gingerly the boys crawled out of the car, fearful of dislodging it from its poised position on the edge of the cliff. Another spray of light burst overhead revealing the road and the hillside with daytime brilliance. Three figures could be seen, far down the road past the foot of the drive, sprinting toward a parked car. They leaped in and sped away.

Sam Radley came running toward the boys. The muscular, sandy-haired detective's face was taut with worry. "You two all right?" he exclaimed.

"Shaken up but okay," Frank said. "What about that masked guy and his pals? Can we go after them?"

Sam shook his head "My car's a quarter of a mile back—I didn't dare park closer. By the time we could get to it, we wouldn't stand a chance of catching them. Better call the police!"

Joe hastily radioed an alarm. Then he hurried

to join his brother and Sam who had gone to untie
Zatta. The one-eyed peddler was unconscious but
bore no visible marks of injury.

"Maybe he fainted," Frank said.

"It's more than that," Sam murmured. "Looks
to me as if he's been drugged."

The operative went off to get his car and
brought it to the spot. They lifted Zatta into the
back seat, then sped to the Bayport General Hospital.

While the unconscious man was being examined, the three sat tensely in the waiting room.

"We really walked into a neat setup," Frank
said. "One of those two guys with the masked man
was standing by Zatta with the lantern. The other
must have been hiding up on the hill, waiting
to sabotage our brakes."

"Right," Joe agreed. "That screen of trees gave
him perfect cover, once we went off to talk to
his partner."

While they waited, the boys gave Sam Radley a
complete account of the events leading up to the
night's excitement. Sam asked, "Do you have the
glass eye with you?"

"Right here." Frank took the eye out of his
pocket and handed it over.

Radley examined it closely. "Hmm. And you
have no idea why Lemuel—or whoever's behind
all this—is so eager to get it back?"

Frank shook his head thoughtfully. "The thing's fairly light. It could be hollow. I've been wondering if something's hidden inside."

Radley held the glass eye close to his ear and shook it. "Nothing rattles. Of course that doesn't prove much. It could be wadded in."

"Trouble is, there's no way to unscrew the eye or pry it apart," Joe remarked. "The only chance to find out would be to break the glass."

Conversation stopped as a white-coated intern came into the waiting room to report on Zatta's condition. "He was definitely drugged," the medic informed Sam and the Hardys. "There's a puncture mark from a hypodermic needle on his right arm. Otherwise he's in good shape, so I think we'll let him sleep it off."

Radley agreed to stand guard in Zatta's room. He told the boys he knew of another operative with whom he could take turns in shifts.

Frank and Joe left the hospital and found a twenty-four-hour service station open a block away. Luckily it had a tow truck available. The boys rode with the mechanic to Shore Road and had him tow their convertible to his garage. The boys walked home.

"That's funny," Joe muttered as he tried to turn his key in the side door.

"What's funny?" Frank asked.

"The lock has been jimmied!" he exclaimed.

The Hardys stared at each other in alarm.

"Whoever did it may still be here!" Frank whispered.

Joe gave his brother a startled look, then hastily pushed the door open and snapped on the light.

The boys began a cautious search of the house, switching on the lights in each room as they went along. The first floor was empty. Tensely they mounted the stairs.

When they came to Aunt Gertrude's room, Frank gave a gasp. "She's gone!"

They dashed to their parents' room. Mrs. Hardy, too, had apparently left the house! The brothers' room was also empty—no figure in hiding. Last, they tried their father's study.

"Oh, great!" Frank groaned. "Dad's safe has been cracked!"

CHAPTER XIII

Airport Vigil

Mr. Hardy's safe door had been blown open. The door hung lopsided and the contents lay strewn about. Frank and Joe rushed to examine the situation.

"Anything missing?" Joe asked.

"Doesn't seem to be," Frank replied.

Joe said worriedly, "I wish we knew what happened to Mom and Aunt Gertrude. You don't suppose they—were kidnapped?"

"No," Frank said. "My hunch is they were lured away by some phony message—to give the safe-cracker a clear field. If they don't come back soon, though, we'd better phone an alarm. Now we'd better check Dad's list of secret papers."

The brothers got this from Mr. Hardy's desk, and when they had gathered up the scattered documents, took inventory. "They're all here," said Frank in relief. Suddenly he exclaimed,

"Wait! Dad stowed some cash in the safe when he left town, but I sure don't see it now!"

"The safecracker probably took it," Joe said, "but I'll bet that's not what he came for."

Frank agreed. "Ten to one he was after the glass eye."

Joe hurried to their garage laboratory and returned, bringing their fingerprint kit. He and Frank dusted the safe carefully but found no traces of prints.

"It has been wiped clean," Joe said in disgust.

Just then they heard a car pull up outside the house. Frank dashed to the window.

"It's a taxi," he reported. "Mother and Aunt Gertrude!"

The boys, vastly relieved, went down to meet them.

"Oh! Thank goodness you're safe!" Mrs. Hardy exclaimed, as first she, then Aunt Gertrude gave Frank and Joe a hug.

Frank said, "We were worried about *you*."

"We received a phone call from a man at about twelve-thirty that you boys had had a car accident over in Riverville," Mrs. Hardy explained. "I knew that wasn't where you planned to go and we were frightened out of our wits."

She said that after taking a taxi to Riverville, she and Aunt Gertrude had been unable to find any trace of the boys. Finally, after checking by telephone with the Bayport police, the women had learned about the Shore Road incident and had returned home at once.

Upon hearing of the blown-out safe, the boys' mother and aunt were greatly upset. Frank telephoned headquarters and gave a full report. It was almost three A.M. when the weary family at last retired for the rest of the night.

"Joe, it's a cinch what happened here at the house and that business on Lookout Hill were all part of the same plan," Frank remarked thoughtfully as the brothers undressed for bed.

"Sure. The timing proves that," Joe agreed.

Frank frowned as he went on, "Lemuel, or the Goggler gang, was out to get rid of us tonight and also seek revenge on Zatta. But I still don't see how the glass eye figures."

"What do you mean?"

"Well, if they're really after the glass eye, they must have sent the safecracker for it in case we hadn't brought the eye along."

Joe stretched out on the bed and clasped his hands under his head. "So?"

"So it doesn't make sense. For all they knew, we had the glass eye with us. And if we'd gone over the cliff, the glass eye would've wound up at the bottom of Barmet Bay."

"Hey, that's right!" Joe sat up. "Then maybe it's *not* the eye they're after!"

Frank took the glass eye out of his trouser pocket and studied it again. "That wouldn't explain the attack on us at the empty house," he reasoned.

"Okay!" Joe exclaimed. "So maybe it *is* the glass eye they're concerned with—but not because it's valuable."

"Then why so much trouble to get hold of it?"

"Because there may be something about it that would incriminate them—evidence that would put the gang behind bars! That way, they'd be just as happy to have it sunk in the bay!"

Frank gave his brother a startled glance. "Joe, you may have hit the answer!" He held the glass eye up to the light. "If there *is* something inside," he speculated, "the opening may have been covered up with the iris. Then the whole thing was glazed over smoothly."

Joe switched off the light and settled back. "When Dad gets home, maybe he'll agree to breaking the eye open."

"Right. In the meantime, I'll keep it under my pillow at night until the safe is repaired."

Exhausted by their strenuous activity, the Hardys slept late Sunday morning and awoke just in time for church. After that, Frank and Joe went to the service station. Their car was ready. They were told that both the hydraulic brake lines and the hand brake cable had been cut.

As they reached home, Mrs. Hardy came out to tell them their father was radioing from St. Louis.

"We'll be right there," Frank said, and dashed inside.

Fenton Hardy listened with keen and worried interest as his sons related everything that had happened since he had left Bayport. "Be on guard at all times, boys," he advised.

The private investigator told Frank and Joe that Ace Pampton, the swindler whom he was after, might be doubling back to Bayport.

"An airline clerk says a man answering Pampton's description bought a ticket to Bayport via New York," Mr. Hardy explained. "He took off on the noon flight. I hate to leave here in case it's a false alarm. So I'd like you boys to cover the airport and keep watch."

"Sure thing, Dad," said Frank. "What does he look like?"

"Medium height—quite bald—and he's been growing a brown beard as disguise. He was wearing a light-blue summer suit and no hat."

"Should be easy to spot," Joe put in. "What time is he due in Bayport?"

"Three-ten if he makes the connection in New York," Mr. Hardy replied. "If he doesn't show up, stick around and watch for the next flight."

"Roger!" Frank acknowledged.

The brothers set off for the Bayport airfield minutes later and arrived at 2:57. Presently a loud-speaker blared:

"Flight 401 from New York is now arriving at Gate 12."

Frank and Joe joined a stream of people hurrying out to the apron to watch the plane discharge its passengers. Suddenly Frank spotted a burly, mash-nosed figure in a chauffeur's uniform.

"Hey, Joe," he muttered, "that's Rip Sinder from the health farm!"

"He must be here to meet a new guest," Joe whispered.

The apelike ex-pug saw them looking at him. He nodded and casually scratched his jaw with an odd gesture, using the forefinger and little finger of his clenched hand.

The Hardys nodded in return and shifted their gaze. The next instant Joe gasped. "Frank!

There's that guy who held up the Bijou!" he exclaimed.

The swarthy, hook-nosed man had been standing just inside the doorway to the terminal building. Apparently he had spotted the Hardys, for he turned and quickly strode away. Meanwhile, the disembarking passengers were already coming down the plane's ramp.

"Go after him, Joe!" Frank said. "I'll keep watch for Pampton!"

Joe darted into the building. The holdup man was disappearing into the crowd. Joe sidestepped and elbowed his way through the jostling throng. But he made little progress. In a moment his quarry was lost from sight.

"Gangway, please!" A skycap was pushing a

hand truck loaded with baggage directly across Joe's path. The boy groaned.

In desperation Joe yelled, "Stop, thief! Stop that man!"

People sprang up from benches to gape in all directions and the crowd began to mill even more excitedly. By the time airport guards made their way to the scene, the whole terminal was in wild confusion.

A thorough search was made, but the dark-complexioned man had vanished. Joe rejoined his brother to report failure. Meanwhile, Frank had seen no sign of Pampton. As they walked up and down outside the terminal building, they saw the health-farm chauffeur, Rip Sinder, drive off. His station wagon was empty.

"Looks as though his man didn't arrive either," Joe remarked glumly.

Two more flights were due from New York that afternoon—one at five-thirty and another at seven-fifteen. The Hardys waited for both. But no one resembling Ace Pampton arrived on either flight.

"Great. This is what I call a well-spent afternoon," Joe grumbled as they drove off.

"Let's stop at the hospital," Frank proposed. "Zatta should be conscious by now."

Joe agreed, eager to learn whatever information the peddler might be able to provide.

The brothers had a quick supper in town, then

went on to the Bayport General Hospital. They took the elevator from the lobby to the fourth floor. Zatta was in Room 410.

The Hardys stopped outside with puzzled frowns. A crudely drawn sign had been taped to the closed door. It showed a hand with the fore and little fingers raised, middle fingers clenched over the thumb.

"What's that supposed to mean?" Joe said.

Suddenly Frank's eyes widened. "That's the same gesture Rip Sinder made at the airport!"

CHAPTER XIV

Sinister Flower Gift

"WHAT gesture?" Joe said to his brother.

"Don't you remember when Sinder nodded to us, the way he scratched his jaw—with two fingers?"

Joe's eyes kindled thoughtfully. "That's right —I do remember now! It could be just a coincidence, though."

"Maybe," Frank said. "Let's find out who put this sign up—and why."

The boys opened the door and went into the room. Sam Radley was watching the doorway warily, but at sight of the Hardys he relaxed and grinned.

"Hi, Sam!" Frank greeted him. "Did you find someone to spell you on guard?"

"Yes, an operative named Vickers—he's worked for your dad before," Radley replied. "I just came on again at four."

Zatta sat propped up in bed, with a black patch

over one eye instead of his usual dark glasses. He had been playing checkers with Sam, and the board lay on the bed beside him. He seemed tense and fearful, and his one good eye stared at Frank and Joe with feverish intensity.

"Hi, Mr. Zatta!" Joe said cheerfully. "Feeling better?"

"Naah! I feel terrible!" the peddler croaked. "If I get out o' this alive, it'll be a miracle!"

Frank shot a questioning glance at Radley. "What about that sign on the door?"

The operative indicated Zatta with a slight jerk of his head. "He wanted it up—drew it himself. Then he raised a rumpus till the nurse agreed to stick it on the door."

"But why?" Joe said.

Radley shrugged. "He wouldn't tell me. Said he'd talk to you fellows or your dad—no one else."

The Hardys turned toward the peddler. The talk about the sign seemed to have stirred up his fears. Zatta's good eye darted anxiously from one to another of the trio.

"Do you feel like talking to us now, Mr. Zatta?" Frank asked gently.

"Sure, I'll talk. I'll tell you everything," the peddler said in a shaky voice. "Come closer so I don't have to speak so loud. . . . Yeah, that's better. . . . Now, about that sign on the door— the hand with the two fingers stickin' out—"

Someone rapped on the door. Zatta broke off with a fearful jerk that sent the checkerboard and checkers clattering to the floor.

Radley strode to the door and opened it—only a crack at first, then wide enough for a nurse to enter. She came into the room holding a large circular bundle wrapped in florist's paper. "For you," she said, handing it to Zatta. Surprised, the peddler tore off the paper, disclosing a wreath of white lilies. Their heavy perfume filled the air with an almost sickly fragrance.

"Lilies!" Zatta screamed. "This—this looks like a funeral piece! Where'd it come from? Who sent it?" He shoved the wreath at the nurse.

She took the wreath with a shocked look. "Well, I—I don't know," she faltered. "The florist's deliveryman brought them up to our station. There's an enclosure card here addressed to you, Mr. Zatta."

She detached a small white envelope from the ribbon on the wreath and handed it to the patient. With trembling fingers he opened it and plucked out the card.

Zatta took one quick look at the card, then let out a hoarse screech. His gaunt frame began to quiver, as if with a sudden chill.

"What is it?" Frank exclaimed. "What's wrong?" He took the card from Zatta's shaking hand. Joe and Radley pressed close to see it.

The card bore the drawing of an eye. It had a catlike oval pupil with zigzag spark lines!

"What does it mean?" Joe gasped. All three looked at Zatta.

"I'm not talkin'!" he whined. "I'm not sayin' another word, see? They almost got me once, but I ain't stickin' my neck out again!"

"Who are *they?*" Frank asked. Seeing the peddler's look of stubborn panic, he pleaded, "You must tell us. How can we find the people who sent this and turn them over to the police if you won't help us?"

But Zatta shrank back in terror, huddling among the bedclothes. "I told you I'm not talkin'! So stop askin' me!" His unpatched eye rolled wildly. "Don't let anyone in here! Lock the windows and lock the door and keep 'em locked!"

Seeing the patient working himself into a frenzy, the nurse hastily called a doctor. Zatta was given sedation and the medic advised the Hardys to break off the interview. Frank and Joe reluctantly went back to their car, leaving Sam Radley on guard.

"What a break! Just when he was going to tell us what that sign meant!" Joe grumbled.

"It's pretty clear what the eye means," Frank said ruefully. "It must be a warning from the same gang that captured him before—probably the Gogglers."

Joe agreed and added, "Those funeral lilies were warning enough, but the eye really sent Zatta up in smoke. That reminds me—the eye drawn under Mrs. Lunberry's window must have been meant as a warning, too, for her not to talk any more to us."

Frank nodded. "It was bound to scare her, even if she didn't know what it meant. For that matter, the guy was probably trying to scare us, too."

As Frank slid behind the wheel of their convertible, he went on, "There's one thing we can check out right now, Joe."

"You mean, who sent the flowers?"

"Right. The card said Barmet Bay Floral Shop."

The two boys drove to the shop, which was near the hospital and remained open on Sundays. They arrived just as the owner was about to close for the evening. Frank explained who the boys were and mentioned the wreath of lilies.

"We'd like to know who sent it."

The shop owner shook his head. "I'm afraid I can't help you, boys—I don't know myself."

"How come?" Joe queried.

"The order was stuck under the door while I was at lunch."

"No name or return address on it?" Frank said.

"No. None on the envelope and none inside. Just a twenty-dollar bill and a printed note saying to send a wreath of lilies to Mr. Henry Zatta at the Bayport General Hospital." The florist scratched his head thoughtfully and added, "Oh, yes. There was something else on the note, too—a funny-looking drawing of an eye. The note asked me to copy that on a gift card and enclose it with the wreath."

"Do you still have the note and the envelope around somewhere?" Joe asked eagerly. "We'd like to see them, please."

"Sorry. They got burned up in the incinerator less than ten minutes ago when I cleaned up."

Frank and Joe thanked the shop owner and went back to their car. They were completely disgusted.

"There goes another good lead," Joe said.

As soon as the Hardys arrived home, they hurried to the basement and warmed up their short-wave radio. Frank sent out a code call and soon made contact with their father, who always carried a small but powerful pocket transceiver with him when traveling. Frank reported the hospital incident and also the fact that no one resembling Ace Pampton had arrived at the airport.

Fenton Hardy was surprised and disappointed. "I can't understand it," he said. "Since I talked to you this afternoon, I've picked up other clues which convinced me the man who bought the airline ticket here *was* Pampton. Of course he may have stopped over in New York. The last lap of his flight may have been a red herring to throw us off his trail."

"Or he may have used the stopover time in New York to disguise himself, Dad," Frank suggested.

"Sure," Joe put in. "He could have gone into the washroom at the airport terminal and changed to different clothes—or maybe even changed his facial appearance in some way."

"That's a thought," the investigator agreed. "The name he used in buying the ticket was Brown—Otto Brown. I should have told you before. Better call the airport and find out if he was on any of those incoming flights from New York."

"Right. We'll check and let you know, Dad," Frank promised.

Joe hurried upstairs to make the telephone call and returned a few minutes later, looking glum. "Pampton fooled us, all right," he reported. "The airline clerk said Otto Brown landed on the three-ten flight."

Mr. Hardy received the news without losing his good humor. "Just one of those setbacks a detective has to expect, boys," he said. "I'll explore his trail here for another day or so. I may turn up a clue to what he's after in Bayport. Keep your eyes open for him."

Next morning Frank and Joe set out for the airport again with the faint hope of tracing Pampton's trail from the terminal. On the way, they stopped off at Bayport Police Headquarters to find out if Chief Collig had anything to report on Malcolm Izmir.

"Yes, I received a written report from the Ocean City chief about half an hour ago. Then I talked to him on the phone. As I told you, Izmir is a respected businessman and quite active in community affairs. But there was one odd discrepancy I noticed."

"What's that?" Frank asked.

"You said he told you he had received a number of threatening messages. If so, he must have clammed up about them to the police—they knew nothing of any such threats." Collig paused to pull an envelope from his drawer. "However, a prowler was caught several days ago, trying to break into his house. Here's a mug shot of him the police sent over."

Collig held out the photograph of a dark-haired, hook-nosed man. Frank and Joe were thunderstruck.

Frank cried out, "That's the Bijou holdup man!"

CHAPTER XV

The Brass Crescent

COLLIG looked hard at Frank. "Are you certain this is the theater thief?" he asked the Hardys.

"Positive," Frank replied. "We spotted the man at the airport yesterday. Joe chased him, but he got away. We thought the airport guards would report it."

"It's possible they did," the chief replied. "I haven't gone over all this morning's reports."

Joe noticed that the name on the photograph was Nick Cordoza. "If he was caught trying to break into Izmir's pace, how come the police didn't hold Cordoza? Joe asked.

"Izmir refused to press charges, so they had to let him go," Chief Collig replied. "Cordoza has a record—he served time for armed robbery—but he wasn't wanted for anything else when they picked him up at Ocean City. However, we'll put out a general alarm for him on the Bijou job."

As the boys came out of headquarters, Frank remarked. "That makes two things about Izmir that need explaining."

"Name them," Joe said.

"First, why didn't he report those threatening letters to the police?"

"Maybe he never got any," Joe theorized. "He may have been lying to us."

"But we know he's frightened," Frank pointed out. "Why else would he have those savage Dobermans? Which brings up the second question," he went on. "Why did Izmir let Cordoza go?"

"Maybe he was afraid of gang revenge," Joe said. "Remember, Cordoza wore a Goggler disguise on the movie holdup."

"Could be," Frank said doubtfully. "But if Izmir's already in fear of his life, what has he got to lose by putting Cordoza behind bars?"

Just then a horn tooted across the street.

"There's Tony Prito," Joe said.

A smart-looking white panel truck made a U-turn during a break in traffic and pulled up behind the Hardys' car.

Tony stuck his head out, grinning proudly. "How do you like our new panel job?"

"A real beauty!" Frank said as the Hardys looked it over. "When did you get it?"

"Saturday. She's not even broken in yet."

"What're you doing with that brass crescent

over the grille?" Joe asked. "You had that on your old panel truck, didn't you?"

Tony chuckled. "Sure—we always mount it on one of our trucks. Dad brought it over from Italy with him as a keepsake. He used it as a hood ornament on the first car he owned."

"What's it supposed to be?" Frank put in.

"It's a *corno*. That means—well, I guess you'd call it an amulet."

"An amulet?" Joe echoed. "You mean, like a lucky piece?"

"That's right. It's for warding off the *malocchio*—the evil eye."

In spite of themselves, Joe and Frank were startled by Tony's remark. Both were reminded instantly of the "blind" peddler's warning: *"Watch out for bad eye!"*

Tony continued, "There are people called *jettatori*, see? That means 'throwers'—they're the ones who have the evil eye. Sometimes they know it and sometimes they don't. But everyone else knows it, or at least the word soon gets around."

"How come?" Frank asked.

"Because these *jettatori* put the double whammy on everyone they look at. For instance, you let a *jettatore* look crooked at you and the next thing you know, you break a leg or come down with measles or flunk your exams!"

The Hardys stared at their friend and shook their heads. Tony burst out laughing.

"Look! I'm not saying I believe it, pals. But a lot of people over in the old country still do—especially around Naples. If they meet a *jettatore,* they make a quick sign to foil the whammy—like, say, the *mano cornuta.*"

Tony held out his hand with the fore and little fingers extended and middle fingers clenched over his thumb. Frank and Joe gaped.

"Hey, relax, you fellows!" Tony exclaimed. "I don't *really* believe you two have the evil eye. Of course Joe does look a bit—"

"What did you call that sign?" Frank broke in.

"The *mano cornuta,*" Tony said, making it again. "It means the 'horned hand.' Why?"

"Jumpin' goldfish!" Joe gasped. "That's the sign Zatta made for his hospital-room door!"

As Tony gave him a baffled look, Joe hastily told him about the one-eyed peddler.

"You mean Zatta is really trying to keep off the evil eye?" Tony inquired.

"He's trying to keep off something, but it may not be the same kind of evil eye you were telling us about," Frank said. "I'll bet this explains what happened at the airport yesterday!"

"How do you mean?" asked Joe.

"You remember that gesture Rip Sinder made, scratching his jaw?"

"You mean when Sinder spotted us he made that 'keep away' sign to warn Nick Cordoza!"

"Could be," Frank said, "but I was thinking of

Ace Pampton. Sinder came to meet *somebody* on that three-ten flight and yet we saw him drive away with his station wagon empty."

"You mean he came to meet Pampton?"

"Yes. Cordoza was inside the terminal and could see us before we saw *him*—he didn't really need a warning to make him scram. But Pampton was coming off the plane and would have to walk right past us. So Rip made the 'keep away' sign to warn Pampton not to approach him. He didn't want us to see the two of them together."

Joe was excited. "That adds up. Pampton walks into the airport building, and Sinder drives off, as if the person he came to meet never arrived."

"Cut out the double-talk, you detectives," Tony pleaded. "What's this all about?"

The Hardys told how they had gone to the airport the day before to keep a watch for the swindler their father was hunting.

"If you're right, Frank, that explains why Pampton came back to Bayport," Joe said. "He was planning to check in at Doc Grafton's Farm—and hide out until the heat's off."

Tony whistled. "Chet will sure have a shock when he hears this!"

"There's a way we may be able to find out quickly," Frank said.

"How?" Joe asked.

"Pampton probably took a taxi out to the health farm."

"So we can check the cab companies!" Joe exclaimed. "Swell idea, Frank!"

"If it works," said Frank, "we'll have your info to thank, Tony."

Their pal grinned. "You two 'private Evil Eyes' go to it! I have to pick up a set of blueprints from an architect."

He gunned the truck's motor, made a U-turn, and sped off down the street.

The Hardys hurried to a phone booth in a nearby drugstore and called each of the three taxicab companies which operated in Bayport. Joe suggested a soda while the dispatchers were checking their drivers' log sheets from the day before. Then Frank called each company again.

On the third call, to the Eagle Cab Service, the dispatcher said:

"Yeah, one of our drivers picked up a fare at the airport at three-fifteen Sunday and drove him out to Doc Grafton's Health Farm."

"Who was the driver?" Frank asked. "Could I get in touch with him?"

"Sure, he's out at the airport right now, in fact. A little man named Mike Doyle. Cab twenty-two. I'll tell him to wait for you."

"Thanks a lot!"

Frank and Joe drove quickly to the airport. They soon found the driver.

"The health farm . . . yesterday afternoon . . . lemme see now." Mike Doyle shoved back his cap and scratched his head. "Oh, sure. I re-member now. A red-haired gent, soft-spoken. Wore big horn-rimmed glasses."

Frank snapped his fingers. "I remember him, Joe! I saw him get off the plane." Turning back to the driver, he said, "Clean-shaven fellow, wasn't he?"

Mike nodded. "That's right. What's he done?"

"If it's the man we're after, he's wanted for swindling," Frank replied.

"Wow!" Mike exclaimed. "Glad I could help."

The two boys sped home excitedly.

"Pampton must have shaved off his beard at the New York air terminal and put on a red wig and glasses," Joe reasoned.

Frank gave a tense nod. "And if Rip Sinder knew Pampton was dodging the law, the health farm may be a regular hideout for criminals!"

Reaching their house, the boys hurried down to the basement and tried calling their father by radio. Luckily he was in his hotel room and re-sponded at once.

Frank informed him of what they had learned, then said, "Dad, Joe and I have a plan we think you should try!"

CHAPTER XVI

The Walking Mummy

FENTON HARDY was eager to hear the boys' plan. "If it's as good as some of the other stunts you two have dreamed up for cracking a case," he told Frank, "I might give it a whirl."

"Well, here goes," Frank began. "If Doc Grafton *is* running a criminals' hideout on the side, you sure can't walk right in and arrest Pampton."

"Probably not," Mr. Hardy agreed. "They may have a clever warning system in case of a raid, and no doubt some foolproof hiding places on the grounds. In fact, Grafton would be crazy not to, if your theory's correct."

"Then it might help if you could case the layout from the inside first. Right, Dad?"

"No doubt about it. What do you suggest?"

Frank said, "By checking into the health farm yourself—say, posing as a tired businessman from St. Louis."

Fenton Hardy was instantly taken with the scheme. To avoid suspicion that he might be a detective on Pampton's trail, Mr. Hardy decided that he would first fly to Cleveland.

"I'll make the arrangements from there over the phone, then hop a plane to Bayport and check in at the health farm under a disguise. I'll call my-self—hmm—let's say, Foster Harlow."

Frank said, "Try to keep in touch with us by radio. We'll tell Chet to be on the lookout, in case you need any help there at the farm."

The talk with their father made both boys eager for another look at Doc Grafton's health resort. Frank also hatched an idea for gleaning further information on Malcolm Izmir.

"Remember what Bill Braxton was telling us about Zachary Mudge on the way to Long Point?" he remarked to Joe.

"You mean about Mr. Mudge being a big wheeler-dealer in the financial world?"

"Right. With his contacts, he could probably find out plenty about Izmir."

Joe gave a puzzled nod. "Maybe so, but what makes you think he'd tell *us*? Businessmen are pretty closemouthed about that sort of thing."

"Usually, but I think I know how we can get Mr. Mudge to help us." As Frank explained his plan, Joe grinned approval.

As soon as lunch was over, the brothers drove

to the health farm. Frank told the gatekeeper who they were and asked if they might see Mr. Zachary Mudge. "It's about a boat he was thinking of buying, called the *Sea Spook*," Frank said.

The gatekeeper relayed their message over the telephone. After a few minutes he received Mudge's reply and turned back to the boys.

"Okay. Mr. Mudge says he'll be waiting for you on the terrace. Go straight up the drive."

On their way up, the Hardys saw Chet heaving a medicine ball back and forth to several guests on the lawn. The men looked cool and relaxed in shorts and summer shirts, but Chet was red-faced and puffing.

Joe grinned as they waved to their chum. "Looks as though poor Chet is getting more of a workout than the patients," he murmured.

Zachary Mudge was pacing with his cane on the stone-flagged terrace, a large cigar clenched between his teeth.

"Finally got here, did you?" He shook hands briskly with the boys. "Took you long enough to get up that hill. Could've made it twice as fast myself."

"I guess we haven't your energy, sir," Frank said with a smile.

Mudge grunted, then followed Joe's gaze toward two men standing near the front door of the building. One was Rip Sinder. The other was a small, foxy-faced man wearing a large diamond ring. They had been watching the Hardys, but as they saw Mudge looking at them, the smaller man broke into a gold-toothed smile and waved.

"Who's that man?" Joe asked.

"That weasely little twerp? He's Doc Grafton, the quack who runs this vegetable farm." Mr. Mudge sneered. "Nosy, too. Let's take a stroll."

The trio walked out across the lawn.

"Now then, what's all this about the *Sea Spook?*" Mudge asked. "The engineer who checked her out says she broke down on the test."

"That's partly what we came to tell you about," said Frank. "Braxton believes she was sabotaged and we think he may be right."

"Y' think so? My man Rummel doubts it."

"Well, we can't prove it," Frank admitted. "But don't forget, Braxton was attacked at his boat-house and knocked unconscious. There may be no connection, but—well, *something* mysterious is going on."

Mudge paused and peered at Frank from under bushy eyebrows. "What're you suggesting, son?"

Frank shrugged. "You remember us mentioning a Mr. Lambert who was interested in the *Spook?*"

"Are you saying he was behind the sabotage?"

"We don't know," Frank said. "We've been doing some investigating, though, and the trail seems to lead to a wealthy businessman over in Ocean City. His name is Izmir."

"Malcolm Izmir?"

"That's right," said Joe. "Do you know him?"

"I've heard the name." The old man's eyes kindled with interest as if he sensed a hint of financial skulduggery. Suddenly Mr. Mudge was right in his element. "Let me get this straight, boys—do you think Izmir could have had the *Spook* sabotaged to keep me from investing money in Braxton's design?"

Again Frank shrugged. "We didn't say that, sir."

But the financier had already made up his mind —exactly as the Hardys had hoped.

"So Izmir thinks he can put one over on me— Zack Mudge, does he?" The old man cackled and thumped his cane on the ground. "Well, we'll see about that. You leave it to me, sonnies. In twenty-four hours I'll know all there is to know about Malcolm Izmir, including what he eats for breakfast!"

The Hardys escorted Mr. Mudge back to the terrace, then said good-by. A smile was twitching at Joe's lips as the brothers started down the drive. He muttered to Frank:

"I'll bet Mr. Mudge is a whirlwind when he goes into action! You sure revved him up with that line you gave him!"

"I didn't say anything that wasn't true," Frank replied. "For all we know, there may *be* some connection between Spotty Lemuel and Izmir."

"Guess we'd better post Chet on the latest," said Joe.

The medicine-ball session was over and Chet was now leading his group of guests in a series of push-ups.

"Eleven-uh . . . twelve-uh . . . Ummh-thirteen -uh . . ." The last came out in an agonized grunt as Chet, beet-red, barely hoisted himself off the ground.

Joe chuckled. "We'd better rescue Chet before he folds up."

He and Frank caught their pal's attention and he quickly struggled to his feet. "That's f-f-fine, gentlemen," he panted. "You're doing great. I hate to interrupt these exercises, but I have to see what these two fellows want. Just keep going, please, or take a short rest period."

Chet trotted gratefully over to join the Hardys.

"Looks as if we came just in time," Frank said.

"Boy, you're not kidding!" Chet mopped his forehead. "Whew! I'm not sure I like this job as well as I thought I would! Handball, water polo, body-building, and now this! And the lunch they feed you wouldn't keep a flea alive. Boy, am I ever sick of cottage cheese and lettuce!"

"You'll be down to a mere two-hundred-pound shadow by the time summer's over," Joe said.

Joe chuckled, "We'd better rescue Chet
before he folds up."

"Lay off, Joe," Frank said with a smile. "Assistant Morton is really earning his salary." He lowered his voice and added, "Listen, Chet, did you see a red-haired man check in here yesterday?"

The stout boy shook his head. "I wasn't here Sunday. Why?"

Joe hastily told their chum about Ace Pampton and their suspicion that the health farm might secretly be a hideout for wanted criminals. Chet's face was a picture of consternation.

"Good grief!" he gulped. "Don't tell me I've got myself mixed up with a nest of crooks! I'm going to quit right now!"

When he learned, however, of the role Mr. Hardy was to play, Chet promised to stick it out and keep his eyes open for the fugitive swindler, as well as to be on the lookout for the detective.

As the two young sleuths drove back to town, Joe remarked, "Do you remember Mrs. Lunberry saying she had seen something like that chalked eye before?"

Frank nodded as he steered the car. "She thought it might have been somewhere in connection with her husband's work. Why?"

"Well, I've been thinking about what Tony told us, and the 'horned hand' picture Zatta put up. Do you suppose that drawing of an eye could represent the evil eye?"

"Maybe. Let's check with Mrs. Lunberry."

The boys drove to their boathouse, took out the *Sleuth*, and headed up the Willow River to Brockton. Mrs. Lunberry was happy to see them and listened eagerly to Frank's report of their visit to Fontana's art shop.

"That really isn't why we came, though," Frank said. "We'd like to know if you've ever heard of a superstition about the evil eye."

"Yes, indeed," Mrs. Lunberry replied. "That's a very old—" Suddenly she broke off in surprise. "Of course! That's what that eye chalked under my window reminded me of!"

She explained that when on digging expeditions with her husband she had often seen similar eyes. "They were carved in mud-brick walls or inlaid in mosaic on ancient ruins."

"You mean people would carve evil eyes on their own houses?" Joe asked, puzzled.

The elderly woman smiled. "It's hard to explain, but Clarence told me once that it's a very common kind of superstitious thinking. The idea is that a harmless form of the thing you're afraid of can help to ward off the real thing."

The boys instantly thought of Zatta and the drawing on the hospital door. Aloud Joe asked, "Is there any chance the evil eye could be connected with the curse on the Jeweled Siva?"

"I'm sure it must be," she said. "Superstitions

about the evil eye have existed in many parts of the world, probably including India."

Mention of the curse seemed to upset Mrs. Lunberry, so Frank changed the subject and asked the woman how she had happened to make arrangements with Fontana to sell the precious idol.

"I wrote to several dealers before making up my mind," Mrs. Lunberry replied. "In the meantime, I was keeping the Siva in a safe-deposit box at the bank. Then one day Mr. Fontana came all the way to Brockton to see me, and I decided to let him handle the sale."

"Did he bring references?" Frank asked. "Or persuade you that he could sell it for the highest price?"

"Nothing like that, I'm afraid." The boys asked for a description, which fit the man they had seen in New York. Mrs. Lunberry smiled. "He seemed like such a nice man. Why, he even took me for a ride in his brand-new car. He'd bought it that very day in Ocean City."

"Not a new Torpedo?" Joe asked sharply.

"Why, yes—I believe that was the make."

The boys were startled but said nothing, about this new development until they were aboard the *Sleuth*, heading downriver.

"This proves to me that Malcolm Izmir, or someone at Izmir Motors, is mixed up in the theft of the Jeweled Siva," Joe declared.

"And maybe Fontana himself," Frank speculated.

That evening Chet Morton stopped at the
Hardys' house in his jalopy and honked his horn
urgently. Frank and Joe rushed outside.

"What's up?" Frank asked.

"Plenty!" The stout youth's eyes were wide with
fear. "I j-just saw a walking mummy!"

CHAPTER XVII

Secret Signals

"A walking mummy?" Joe echoed. Then he grinned. "Seems to me I recall we were going to be kidnapped once. What's the joke this time?"

"It's no joke!" Chet retorted indignantly. "I tell you I saw a walking mummy!"

"Okay, okay. Where?" Frank asked.

"At the health farm, that's where. It was all on account of you guys, too."

"How come?" Joe said.

Chet explained that he had had no luck in finding out if a new guest had checked in at the health resort on Sunday, nor had he seen anyone answering Ace Pampton's description. And so he had purposely hung around on the job until long after his usual quitting time.

"I figured I might be able to do some snooping while dinner was being served," Chet went on. "There was one particular building I wanted to get a look at."

"Which one?" Frank put in.

"I don't think you fellows have seen it. An old, two-story frame building, set back among the trees on the north side of the grounds."

"What's special about it?" Joe asked.

"The place is always kept locked. I've seen only one other person at the farm besides Doc Grafton and Rip Sinder ever go in there—in fact, today Doc told me it was off limits."

Frank and Joe looked at each other with rising excitement.

"Well, go on! What happened?" Joe urged as Chet paused to munch a candy bar.

"For Pete's sake, don't rush me!" Chet retorted. "I'm half starved. I haven't even had dinner yet."

He went on, "Anyhow, I thought I'd try to peek inside, so I sneaked up through the trees. And then all a sudden this—this mummy walked past the window!" Chet's face turned paler at the recollection. "The—the head was all wound around with bandages!"

The stout boy shuddered and his voice shook with fear. Joe tried to reassure him. "Easy, Chet! You've been seeing too many horror movies, like 'The Creature from the Tomb'!"

"This was worse than any movie!"

"Who's the other person allowed into the building?" Frank asked Chet.

"Some old man named Dr. Vardar. He's the health-farm physician."

Joe chuckled. "Chet, I think you've been working too hard out there."

"Okay. Don't believe me." The stout boy gunned his engine. "Count me out of this case!" he exclaimed. "You two can investigate that creepy joint alone next time!"

"Come on, Chet," Frank said soothingly. "We appreciate your help. You can't back out now. Dad might arrive at the farm any time."

Somewhat mollified, Chet consented, and a moment later the yellow jalopy roared off.

Frank and Joe gazed after it. Both were mystified at Chet's story. "I'd like to have a look at that 'mummy' myself," said Joe.

"Me too. But we'd better wait until we hear from Dad."

Shortly before ten o'clock that evening a loud buzz from the basement announced an incoming call over the Hardys' short-wave. Frank and Joe hurried down to receive it.

"Fenton calling Elm Street!" a low voice crackled from the speaker.

"Elm Street to Fenton," Joe responded over the microphone. "We read you. Come in, please."

"Hi, fellows!" said Mr. Hardy. "Just wanted to let you know that I arrived safely."

"You're at the farm now?" Frank put in.

"Right. I flew in on the eight-forty-five plane from Cleveland, got picked up by the chauffeur, and checked in under the name I gave you. This is the first chance I've had to get in touch. I'm calling from my room."

The boys quickly reported Chet's story.

"Good lead. I'll follow it up." Mr. Hardy's voice dropped to a whisper. "I think someone's coming. Over for now!"

Late that night Frank awoke from a sound sleep. He lay drowsily for a few moments, wondering what had aroused him. Suddenly he became aware of a muffled clicking sound.

"Where's that coming from?" Frank wondered.

He sat bolt upright in bed. The clicking sounds seemed to fade out. Puzzled, Frank lay back on his pillow. At once the clicks became louder!

"Under my pillow!" Frank realized.

He pulled it aside and the clicks became still louder and clearer. Something on the bed glittered in the moonlight streaming in. The glass eye! Frank snatched it up with a stifled cry and held it to his ear.

The clicks were coming from the glass eye!

"Joe! Wake up!" he exclaimed, switching on his table lamp.

His brother raised up sleepily from his bed across the room. Joe blinked in the sudden glare. "Wh-what's up?" he muttered.

"Signals are coming over this glass eye!" Frank whispered. "There must be a miniature receiver inside! Sounds like Morse code!"

As Joe came dashing across the room, Frank held out the eye so his brother could hear it. In a moment the signals ceased.

"Did you get anything?" Joe asked.

"Numbers and letters—but they didn't make any sense to me, offhand," Frank replied.

"Maybe there'll be more!" Joe hastily got pencil and paper from his desk.

The signals began again. The transmission seemed slow and amateurish, and Joe copied down the message easily. It read:

12PM 4112N 7059W 13K 080 1227

As the glass eye fell silent, the Hardys stared at the numbers and letters in puzzlement.

"Get anything out of it?" Joe asked.

"Not much," Frank admitted. "The 'twelve PM' must stand for a time—twelve o'clock midnight. The rest looks like some sort of secret code."

Abruptly the glass eye resumed its ticking. Joe again copied down the Morse signals and found that the same set of numbers and letters were being repeated. While the boys were excitedly discussing the mysterious message, another transmission began with the same contents.

"Frank, that 'N' and 'W' could stand for 'North' and 'West,' " Joe mused. "Maybe a position."

"Right! In latitude and longitude!" Frank exclaimed. "That would be forty-one degrees, twelve minutes north latitude and seventy degrees, fifty-nine minutes west longitude."

"Let's see where that is." Joe bounced up from his chair and strode to a map of the world which the boys had tacked to one wall. His finger traced out the nearest parallel and meridian. "Well, what do you know! It's in the Atlantic Ocean—about halfway between Montauk on Long Island and Nantucket Island, Massachusetts."

"In that case, it must be a ship's position," Frank reasoned. "But what about the last part?"

The Hardys stayed up for another hour, puzzling over the message, but could deduce nothing further. The radio signals being picked up by the glass-eye receiver had long since stopped when the two young sleuths finally went back to bed. It was two o'clock.

Early the next morning Chief Collig telephoned the Hardy home. "I have a follow-up on Izmir that may interest you fellows," he said when Joe answered. "Last night two more men tried to break into Izmir's estate. His watchdogs trapped them and both were caught."

"Who are they?" Joe asked eagerly.

"Their names are Kane and Yaddo. They're both dangerous hoods with police records."

"What's their story?"

"They have none. Neither one will talk."

"Does Izmir know them?" Joe inquired.

"The Ocean City police couldn't tell me that,"

Collig replied. "It was some servant on the estate who turned them in. Yesterday morning Izmir left for New York to go on a European vacation cruise."

"That's right—I'd forgotten," Joe replied. He frowned for a moment, then added, "Just for the record, are you sure he did leave?"

The police chief chuckled. "I thought you might ask me that, so I called the shipping line in New York and checked. Izmir definitely sailed on the *Cristobal* yesterday afternoon."

"Okay. Thanks a lot for letting us know."

Joe relayed the information to his brother as the two boys sat down to breakfast. The morning newscast was just coming on over the Hardys' portable television set. The family grew silent at the announcer's first words.

"A late bulletin states that a prominent East Coast businessman has been lost at sea. The ocean liner on which he had embarked Monday on a Scandinavian cruise, the *Cristobal*, reported by radio that Mr. Malcolm Izmir of Ocean City was missing this morning. His cabin had not been slept in, and he is presumed to have fallen or jumped overboard sometime during the night."

CHAPTER XVIII

News of a Racket

FRANK and Joe were stunned by the news flash on Izmir's disappearance. As they looked at each other in amazement, Frank's eyes suddenly kindled with suspicion.

"Lost at sea!" he exclaimed to his brother. "Are you thinking the same thing I am?"

"Probably. This could have something to do with that message we picked up on the glass eye last night!"

"Message? Glass eye?" Aunt Gertrude darted an inquisitive glance at the boys. "What's all this nonsense?"

"The glass eye started talking last night, Aunty," Frank explained with a wink at his mother.

Miss Hardy's voice was barbed with suspicion. "Are you trying to scare me, young man?"

"No. It's on the level. That glass eye must have a miniature radio receiver inside it. Last night Joe and I heard it picking up signals in Morse—"

The telephone jangled in the hallway. Joe bounded up from the table to answer it.

"Are you one of the Hardy boys?" someone asked in a croaking voice.

"Yes, sir. Joe Hardy. Is this Mr. Mudge?"

"Certainly, I'm Mudge! Zachary Mudge. Who do I sound like?"

"Well, nobody, sir. That is, I mean—"

"Never mind nattering at me!" Mudge rapped out. "I have news for you two. On Izmir."

"Malcolm Izmir?" Joe was startled.

"Yes, Malcolm Izmir." The elderly man added in a burst of exasperation, "Do you know of any other Izmir we've been talking about?"

Joe grinned. "No, sir. It's just that I—"

"Then stop talking so much. You think I have nothing better to do than waste my time answering tomfool questions?" Mr. Mudge seemed to pause for breath and then rattled on, "Now, listen. If you and your brother want to hear what I have to say, you'd better get up here right away. Understand? . . . Can't talk over these phones at the vegetable farm. Probably ears flapping all over the line."

"Right, sir," Joe said. "We'll drive right over."

The Hardy boys hastily finished their bacon and eggs under a barrage of questions from their mother and Aunt Gertrude, then backed their convertible out of the garage and took off.

"Wonder if Doc Bates' office would be open yet," Frank remarked as they sped down Elm Street.

"Sure, I guess so—it's after nine," Joe said with a glance at his wristwatch. "He'd see us, even if it wasn't. But why?"

"I've been wondering if he might be able to tell us anything about that Dr. Vardar who Chet mentioned last night."

"Good idea," Joe agreed. "Let's stop off and ask him."

Dr. Bates, the Hardys' family physician, had his office at home, a rambling stone house a few blocks from Elm Street. The boys found the office entrance open, and the secretary-nurse allowed them to see the doctor at once. Frank explained why they had come.

"Hmm. Dr. Vardar." The physician frowned thoughtfully. "Seems to me I've heard the name, and yet he's not a member of our local medical society. I can look him up in the medical directory and inquire about him later on today."

"That'll be fine, Doctor," Frank said. "Thanks a lot."

The Hardys drove on to the health farm. After stopping at the gatehouse, they were told to walk on up to the main building. Zachary Mudge was pacing the terrace with his cane.

"Half an hour it took you," the elderly financier complained. "I'd still be grubbing for small

change if I moved as slowly as you young whippersnappers move these days."

"Sorry, sir," Frank said, deciding it would be
better not to mention their stop at Dr. Bates'
office. "We're eager to hear what you've learned
about Malcolm Izmir."

Mudge shot a glance over his shoulder at Rip
Sinder, who appeared to be watering some potted
plants on the terrace. "There's ape man over
there, dying for an earful. Got so he follows me
around like a confounded lap dog. Probably
hoping for a tip on the stock market." Mr. Mudge
broke into a pleased cackle. "I gave him a bum
steer on Consolidated Steel yesterday, just for
kicks. Anyhow, let's move on."

They strolled off across the lawn toward the
tennis courts, where several guests were lobbing
balls back and forth.

"Had a call from New York this morning, just
before I phoned you," Zachary Mudge began. "My
man there gave me the whole picture on Izmir."

"He has quite a financial empire, doesn't he?"
Frank asked.

"He did have," Mudge said. "Got his finger in
a dozen or more pies. His different companies and
enterprises are all linked together under a setup
called the Izmir Syndicate. But here's the rub—the
whole structure's about to tumble down around
his ears."

"You mean he's gone broke?" Joe asked in surprise.

"I don't know if *he's* gone broke, but the Izmir Syndicate certainly has," Mudge replied. "My agent says it's near bankruptcy. Apparently Izmir's been defrauding his investors and rigging the books for the past year or so. Now the government's on his trail and he's likely to wind up behind bars."

The elderly financier rubbed his hands gleefully. "If Izmir was interested in the *Sea Spook*, more than likely he was hoping to float a new company and raise a packet of money on the strength of Braxton's hydrofoil design. But just let him try it now! I'll soon cut him down to size!"

"You won't have to, sir," Frank said. "Izmir was lost at sea last night from an ocean liner."

Mudge stopped short and stared at the boys as Frank told him about the news flash. "Well, well, well. Can't say I'm surprised. Man gets in his position, I dare say jumping overboard seems like the best solution."

The Hardys considered this gruesome thought as they walked back toward the terrace with Zachary Mudge. The boys noted a tall man in swim trunks with a towel draped around his neck, striding across the lawn. Apparently he was returning from a swim in the outdoor pool. He was gray-haired, wore glasses, and had rather prominent teeth.

Joe looked at him casually and caught a wink. Then he did a quick double-take and exchanged a startled glance with Frank.

"Did you see who that swimmer was?" Joe asked his brother later, as they started down the drive.

Frank nodded. "Dad—or rather, Foster Harlow. Pretty neat disguise! Those phony teeth and the dyed hair changed his appearance completely."

Joe suggested that they stop off at the Bayport General Hospital and check on Zatta. Sam Radley opened the door of the peddler's room in answer to their knock.

"You two got here at just the right time," Sam muttered as they entered. "I've been working on Zatta. I think he's about ready to talk."

The one-eyed man regarded the Hardys fearfully as they advanced toward his bed.

"How about it, Mr. Zatta?" Frank said. "Don't you think it would make sense to tell us what you know? I promise you the police will give you complete protection from the men who tried to kill you. The sooner you cooperate, the sooner those thugs can be put behind bars."

The peddler gulped and ran his tongue nervously over his lips. "All right," he rasped. "I sure can't stay holed up here for the rest of my life."

His eyes darted over his three listeners. "You guys ever heard o' the Goggler gang?"

The Hardys and Sam Radley nodded.

"The Goggler gang is what the *newspapers* call 'em," Zatta went on. "Guys in the rackets call 'em the Evil Eyes or the Bad Eyes."

"How come?" Joe asked.

Zatta shrugged. "Who knows? Maybe on account o' them eyeballs and glasses they wear when they pull a job. Anyhow, that name ain't no joke —they're bad medicine. Every other mob on the East Coast is scared to death of 'em."

"What about that horned hand you stuck up on the door?" Frank put in.

Zatta flushed. "That's a 'lay off' sign they use. They're in the protection racket, too, see? Every merchant who buys protection from 'em has a sign like that showin' somewhere in his shop. And there ain't a hood dumb enough to touch a place when he sees that hand 'cause he knows the Bad Eyes would carve him up in a hurry if he tried muscling in. I figured if I stuck one of 'em signs up on my door, they'd think I was keepin' my mouth shut and leave me alone."

"Who's the head of the mob?" Radley demanded.

"Nobody knows. I don't even think the Bad Eyes themselves know who their boss is. All I heard is they work for some really hush-hush setup called the Eye Syndicate."

"Okay. Now how about that card you gave us for Dad?" Frank inquired.

"It's like this," the peddler explained. "I been hearin' rumors that something big was about to pop with the Bad Eyes. I don't know whether it's a job they're plannin' to pull or trouble in the gang or what. Anyhow, I spotted one o' the Bad Eyes right here in Bayport."

Joe tried a random shot. "Spotty Lemuel?"

"That's right." Zatta looked at the two boys in astonishment. "I didn't know you kids were wise. When I saw Spotty, I figured the tip might be worth something to your old man. I tried to phone him and got no answer. Then I heard some kids talkin' about you two bein' in that high school game, so I went lookin' for you at the ball field."

Later, Zatta went on, he had heard a remark passed in a dive frequented by gangsters and hoodlums that the Bad Eyes were mixed up in a job involving Fontana's art shop. So he had decided to keep watch on the place in the hope of picking up a further lead.

"But someone must have spotted you two talkin' to me," the peddler ended, "because that night two hoods cornered me and took me for a ride. You know what happened after that."

Leaving Sam Radley on guard, Frank and Joe went down to the hospital lobby and telephoned Collig. The chief promised to send a squad car to the hospital at once and to keep the peddler in protective custody until the case was cleared up.

As the brothers walked out to their car, Frank remarked, "I'll bet the man who spotted us talking to Zatta was Fontana himself."

Joe nodded. "And try this for size. What if the Eye Syndicate is the same as the Izmir Syndicate? The word 'eye' standing for the letter 'I' in Izmir —get it?"

"I get it," Frank said excitedly. "Joe, I believe you've hit the nail right on the head. What say we take the *Sleuth* out on the bay and talk this over? Maybe we can come up with a few more answers if we think it all out!"

"Swell idea!"

The two boys drove to the harbor. As they walked toward the boat dock, Bill Braxton hailed them excitedly.

"Just the guys I'm looking for!" he exclaimed.

"What's up?" Joe inquired.

"I have a new mystery for you two to solve!"

CHAPTER XIX

The Figure at the Window

"A NEW mystery?" Frank said wryly. "We have our hands full now! But let's hear it!"

"Someone took the *Sea Spook* out of her shed last night," Braxton informed the boys.

"You mean she was stolen?" Joe asked, wide-eyed.

"Well, let's say borrowed. That's the funny part of it. She's back in her berth right now. But I'm sure she was taken out during the night."

"How come?" Frank said.

"For one thing, the lock on the waterside door was busted. For another, the bilge is full of sea water—and she was dry as a bone when I left here yesterday."

Intrigued, the two boys eagerly accompanied Bill Braxton to his boathouse. Here they boarded the hydrofoil. Its afterdeck was still wet. Bill also showed them a tin dish from the locker.

"This was on the chart bench," he explained. "Someone used it as an ash tray. You can still see the stain. The person probably emptied it over the side and gave it a quick wipe-off, but I found a stray butt that fell on the deck."

"If the bilge is full," Frank said thoughtfully, "your boat must have shipped a lot of water. Would she do that on the bay?"

Braxton shook his head. "Not a chance. It was calm as a millpond last night. The only way that could happen would be in a fairly heavy swell—maybe along the coast somewhere."

"Did you check with the Coast Guard?" Joe suggested.

Braxton snapped his fingers. "That's a thought." He climbed out onto the catwalk, strode to his desk, and picked up the telephone. After calling the Barmet Bay Coast Guard Station, he hung up and turned back to the Hardys. "Well, that cinches it. Their lookout saw the *Spook* sail out of the bay around ten o'clock last night. The watch that came on at midnight is off duty now, so they're not sure when my boat returned."

Frank and Joe exchanged excited glances.

"How about the fuel tanks?" Joe asked.

"I think they're down a bit, but I'm not positive what the level was when I left," Braxton replied. "That wouldn't tell us much about the range, anyhow. Whoever took the *Spook* could

have filled her tanks and burned it all up before
he brought her back."

"Have you a chart of the coast around Nantucket?" Frank asked. "I'd like to see it."

"Sure." Bill Braxton climbed back aboard and
led the way into the cabin. He removed a chart
from a drawer and spread it out on the bench.

Frank fingered a spot about midway between
Montauk and Nantucket. "Would your tanks
have enough capacity to get the *Spook* there and
back?"

Bill nodded. "Sure. Easy."

"How long would the run take—say at top
speed?" Frank inquired.

"Three hours each way. Maybe less—say two
and a half if I really opened her up and didn't
run into any heavy seas. Why?"

"Joe and I have the same wild hunch, I think."
Frank told about the news report that Malcolm
Izmir had been lost overboard from the *Cristobal*, and also about the mysterious radio signals
he and Joe had picked up over the glass-eye receiver. "Izmir's loss overboard at sea could have
been faked to get him out of a financial jam,"
Frank reasoned. "Someone could have taken your
hydrofoil, picked Izmir up near the *Cristobal*,
and brought him back to shore."

"And the 'someone' could have been Lemuel,"
Joe added. "That would explain why he pre-
tended to be interested in buying the *Spook* and

then never showed up again. All he really wanted was for you to take him out on the bay and show him how to operate this job."

Bill Braxton was stunned. "Could be, all right," he said slowly. "But to pull a trick like that, Izmir would need the cooperation of the master and crew of the *Cristobal*, wouldn't he? That's pretty hard to swallow."

Frank was not so sure of this. "Would you, by any chance, know who owns the *Cristobal*?"

Braxton shook his head.

"Never mind," Frank said. "We'd better notify the police, anyhow, and see if they can lift any fingerprints off the *Spook*."

All three climbed off the hydrofoil and Frank telephoned Chief Collig. He reported the overnight theft of the *Sea Spook* and obtained the name of the company the chief had called to inquire about Izmir's sailing.

"Thanks, Chief." Frank hung up and turned back to the others. "He's sending a detective right over. Joe, let's blast off for home. I have an idea I'd like to follow up."

Driving back to Elm Street, Frank explained, "The *Cristobal* is owned by the Trans-Ocean Line. Dad handled a case for them once, rounding up a gang of card sharks, remember? I think they should be willing to help us."

As soon as they arrived home, Frank made a telephone call to the office of the Trans-Ocean

Line in New York. After listening to his story, an executive of the company assured him that Captain Rowley, the master of *Cristobal*, had a long, spotless record of service. He could be considered above suspicion. The executive promised, however, to call the liner by radiotelephone and arrange a short-wave interview between the Hardys and the captain. Within an hour, the boys made contact.

"When was Izmir last seen, sir?" Frank asked him.

"Soon after midnight last night," Captain Rowley replied. "He came up on the bridge and chatted with the officer on watch."

"What about?"

"Oh, the usual things passengers talk about. He asked the ship's position and course, what the weather outlook was, and so on."

Frank glanced excitedly at Joe. "What *was* the ship's position, sir?"

"Hold on a moment." A short while later Rowley's voice came back on. "Our midnight fix put us at forty-one degrees, twelve minutes north latitude and seventy degrees, fifty-nine minutes west longitude."

Joe had a sudden inspiration. "Could you give us your course and speed at that time, sir?" he put in eagerly.

"According to the log, our course was 080, speed thirteen knots."

"Is there any indication that Izmir went back to his cabin after that?" Frank asked.

"Apparently not, since his bed wasn't slept in, although we don't know," Rowley replied. "He may have fallen over the rail or jumped right after leaving the bridge."

The Hardys thanked the captain and signed off.

"I'd say that's it, Joe!" Frank exclaimed. "The midnight position was the same as the one we picked up over the glass eye!"

"And the next two groups in the message tell the ship's speed and course," Joe pointed out.

Frank went on breathlessly, "And the last numbers—twelve twenty-seven—could be the time Izmir went over the side. Knowing the *Cristobal's* course and speed, Lemuel could plot the exact spot where Izmir jumped."

"Right. But did he stay afloat until the *Spook* arrived?"

"He probably had a life jacket, or even an inflatable raft," Frank guessed. "It would be risky, all right, but not *too* risky if Izmir felt he was in a real jam and might wind up facing a long prison term."

"Sure," Joe agreed. "He and Spotty could easily have figured out beforehand, from the *Cristobal's* sailing time, about where she'd be around midnight. All Izmir had to do was radio his exact position and shine a flashlight every so often. The *Spook* could have picked him up in fifteen minutes."

Just then Mrs. Hardy called to her sons that Dr. Bates was on the phone. Frank hurried from the basement to answer, with Joe close at his heels.

"I've just found out about Dr. Vardar," the medic reported. "He was a prominent plastic surgeon in New York City up until two years ago. Then he became involved in some sort of scandal. I couldn't find out the details, but his license was revoked for malpractice."

"Thanks a lot, sir. That tells us all we need to know." Frank hung up and turned excitedly to his brother, who had been listening in. "Did you get that? Vardar was a plastic surgeon!"

"No wonder Chet thought he saw a mummy!" Joe replied. "Vardar must have operated on someone's face and the patient was still wrapped in bandages."

"Do you realize what that means?" Frank said. "Doc Grafton's Health Farm isn't just a hideout for criminals on the run—it's even a place where they can buy a new face. What a racket!"

Joe's eyes narrowed. "That malpractice bit just gave *me* an idea, Frank."

"Like what?"

"Remember Tony said the Italian name for the evil eye is *malocchio?*"

"So?"

"Well, *mal* must mean 'bad' or 'evil.' And if you shorten Malcolm Izmir's name to one syllable plus a letter, you get 'Mal I.' That could be where the gang got its name—the Evil Eyes!"

"Wow! We're really hot today!" Frank said, socking his fist into his palm. "I'll bet anything the *Sea Spook* brought Izmir back to Bayport and he's hiding out at the health farm right now, getting his face changed!"

"Great, but all this is just theory," Joe reminded his brother. "We have no proof."

"Right," said Frank. "But if Dad can get a peek inside that building Chet told us about, he may be able to wrap up the case. Let's see if we can raise him on the radio!"

The boys hurried back downstairs and tried to contact their father by short-wave, but got no response. After lunch they tried again without success. They continued calling throughout the afternoon, but Mr. Hardy failed to answer. By dinnertime Frank and Joe were worried.

"Let's find out if Chet knows anything," Frank suggested.

He telephoned the Morton farm and hung up a few moments later with a shrug of disappointment. "Chet's mother says he doesn't finish work this evening till nine o'clock. I don't want to risk a phone call to him at the health farm."

"Listen. If we can't reach Dad by that time," Joe said, "let's go meet Chet and do a little scouting."

"Okay with me."

Soon after nine o'clock Chet came ambling through the arched gateway of the health farm. A slight honk drew his attention to the Hardys' parked convertible. He trotted over.

"Hi, fellows!" he exclaimed. "I thought Iola was coming to pick me up."

"We volunteered," Frank said. "Hop in."

As the car drove off, the Hardys gave Chet a quick fill-in. "I think your dad's okay," he assured them. "I saw him. He gave me a wink. Otherwise, I wouldn't have known him."

"What time was that?" Joe asked.

"Around five-thirty. Just before chow."

"Let's try him again," Frank said hopefully.

He pulled over to the side of the road and Joe beamed out a call over their short-wave. This time Fenton Hardy responded. After hearing their story, he said, "Good work, boys. I've already got hold of a key to that building and I'm going to try slipping in after lights-out at ten P.M. But it may be dangerous. Think you fellows could climb over the fence?"

"Sure. What do you want us to do?" Joe said.

"Keep watch for a signal—just in case I run into any trouble."

"Roger!"

Chet was nervous but agreed to help. The boys waited until after ten o'clock, then parked the convertible on the north side of the wooded estate. Scaling the fence, they made their way silently among the trees toward the suspicious two-story frame building. The health farm lay shrouded in darkness. Other than faint gleams from a few shaded windows, most lights on the estate were out. Only the chirping of crickets broke the silence.

"Seen any sign of your dad?" Chet whispered as the three youths joined one another after circling the building.

"Not yet," Frank murmured.

Suddenly they heard the noise of a violent scuffle inside the house—then a muffled cry! The boys' hearts thudded. A light flashed on in an unshaded upper-story window.

"Good grief! What happened?" Joe exclaimed.

Fearing for his father's safety, Frank darted closer to the building. Joe and Chet followed. All paused in the shadow of a dead, gnarled elm tree.

"I'm going to take a peek in the window!" Frank whispered. He scooped up a stone. "Also try to find out with this who's up there. Give me a boost, Joe. Chet, you watch the door!"

Joe laced the fingers of his hands together for Frank to step on, then gave him a quick hoist. Frank grabbed a tree limb and swung himself upward. Meanwhile, Chet had crept to a position which gave him a clear view of the front door.

Frank hurled the stone at the lighted window. *Crash!* Chunks of glass from the broken pane tinkled to the ground. The next moment a figure stepped into sight at the sill—a thick-necked man wearing a dressing gown. He was partly silhouetted against the light, but Frank recognized him.

Malcolm Izmir!

At that instant the door of the house burst open! Two men came rushing out!

Chet hastily retreated, but stumbled over a rock and fell. Scrambling up, he fled toward the trees and shrubbery.

"Get him!" yelled one of the men.

Frank slid down the tree trunk and he and Joe dashed to their pal's aid. As the men whirled, the Hardys tackled them full force. But the man who had not spoken thrust the boys back with the force of a battering ram, then seized them in a crushing grasp. His partner now dealt the brothers several stunning blows.

"Inside!" he snapped. "Quick!" Squirming and kicking, the Hardys were dragged into the building.

Their captors were Spotty Lemuel and Rip Sinder!

Lemuel's lips twisted in a cruel sneer. "Now you'll get the same treatment your father got—in our steam room!"

CHAPTER XX

Mystery Madhouse

SINDER released Frank and Joe, but the ex-pug stood glaring at them watchfully, his huge hands clenching and unclenching.

"You can't get away with this!" Joe panted. "Our friend will have the police here in two minutes!"

Lemuel's eyes glittered in his pale face. "Don't kid yourself, junior! The fence around this joint is electrified—and Sinder turned on the juice as soon as we spotted you punks." He gestured toward a wall switch. "Your buddy will sizzle the second he tries to climb out!"

Frank and Joe went white with fear at the thought. They were in the vestibule of a gloomy, high-ceilinged hallway which appeared to split the large, rambling house into two wings.

"Okay, upstairs, both of you!" Lemuel ordered. He gestured toward a steep staircase just beyond the vestibule. "And no funny business! We'll be right behind you, every step of the way!"

The Hardys obeyed, but their minds were working at top speed. As they mounted the stairs, side by side, they could hear Sinder and Lemuel clumping behind them.

Suddenly Frank sagged, as if still stunned from the blows he had received. He seemed to miss his footing, and sprawled wildly against the steps.

"Hey, on your feet, punk, before I crease your skull!" Lemuel snarled. The gangster prodded Frank with his foot.

Frank moved like lightning. His hands grabbed Lemuel's upraised foot while the man was still off balance and jerked it high in the air! With a scream the man went flying down the staircase!

Sinder grunted with rage and tried to seize Frank, but Joe whirled and gave him a terrific kick on the shoulder. The thug toppled backward, wide-eyed with terror. He clawed vainly for the stair rail, but rolled, thumping and pounding, down the full flight.

"Come on, Joe!" urged Frank, springing to his feet.

The boys bounded to the top of the stairs. The upper hallway was dark and lined with doors. Frank and Joe ran through it, heading toward the rear of the building. Joe suddenly spotted a side passage on their right.

"This way!" Joe hissed, tugging his brother's

sleeve. As they turned, they could hear confused sounds coming from the stairwell.

The passage connected to another corridor. Frank sighted a flight of steps leading downward and steered his brother toward it. "We must get back to that switch and turn off the electricity to the fence!" he whispered hoarsely.

The brothers plunged down the stairs to the first floor, then along a corridor that turned right and opened into the main hallway. It appeared empty and the Hardys raced along. They could hear pounding steps on the second floor, fading toward the rear.

"Whew! Let's hope we're not too late!" Joe breathed as they darted into the vestibule.

Frank flicked off the fence power switch.

"If only we could find Dad!" Joe muttered. "This place is like a maze!"

"Maybe Izmir will tell us!" Frank headed back to the stairs, with Joe at his heels, and ran lightly up the steps.

This time, instead of going straight through the second-floor hall, they turned toward the front of the house. A connecting corridor branched both ways. The Hardys followed it to the right.

Suddenly Frank grabbed Joe's arm and pointed to a doorway at the corner of the hall. A thin line of light seeped out below the door.

"That's the room I saw from the tree," Frank explained in a whisper. "Izmir's in there!"

The boys crept closer. Frank put his hand gently on the knob and flung the door open.

Inside, Malcolm Izmir was standing at a bureau, putting a small jeweled ivory figure into a pouched money belt. He whirled and his jaw dropped in surprise.

Before he could cry out, Joe snatched a pillow from a bed near the door and flung it at him. Izmir ducked, but the pillow caught him in the face. In a split second the Hardys were on him like tigers!

Frank crooked an arm around the startled man's neck and threw him heavily to the floor. Joe knelt on top of him, pinioning Izmir with knees and hands. Meanwhile, Frank poised a hard-knuckled fist directly over Izmir's face. "One yell out of you and—" he warned. "Just tell us where we can find the steam room."

"Second floor back," Izmir croaked. "Last door to the left—main hallway!"

"Tear up some sheets, Joe. Quickly!" Frank ordered. "We'll tie him up!"

In a few minutes the fugitive lay bound and gagged. The boys hurried from the room, and dashed back to the main hallway. At the end, Frank opened the last door on the left. A glare of light dazzled their eyes.

"Dr. Vardar's operating room!" Joe exclaimed.

The white-gowned surgeon stood at an operating table on which a patient lay outstretched. Another man in white, evidently the doctor's assistant, stood near the foot of the table. Both wore surgical masks. Above these, their eyes stared in complete astonishment at the Hardys.

Frank slammed the door before either man could make a move. "Izmir tricked us!"

The boys fled down the back stairs. They could hear running footsteps now in several parts of the house. "We *must* find Dad!" Frank said grimly.

Desperately he and Joe dashed down a rear hallway. At the end of the corridor were a pair of swinging doors. The boys burst through them and stopped short with exclamations of horror.

A row of steam cabinets stood along one wall of the white-tiled room. From one cabinet protruded the head of a gray-haired man. It was drooping to one side. His eyes were closed and his red face was dripping with perspiration.

"Dad!" Frank cried in a choked voice.

While Joe turned off the steam, Frank quickly opened the front of the cabinet and raised the top flaps so they could pull out the unconscious investigator. He had been thrust inside fully clothed, his arms tied behind him.

"Look at this lump on his head," Joe said. "They must have knocked him out first!"

The boys untied their father's hands, then Frank got some cold water from a nearby basin and bathed the detective's head. After the brothers had worked over him for a few minutes, Mr. Hardy began to regain consciousness. Soon he was able to talk and stand up. Frank and Joe briefed him quickly on all that had happened.

"Thanks, boys," the detective said tensely. "I couldn't have lasted much longer in there."

"You won't last much longer—period!" a voice snarled. The three Hardys whirled in dismay as a group of men burst into the room.

At their head was a small, foxy-faced individual clutching a gun. With him were Lemuel, Sinder, and Dr. Vardar's surgical assistant.

"Better not try anything, Grafton," said Fenton Hardy in a taut voice. "Your number's up. You won't stand a chance of getting away."

Doc Grafton's face twisted into a gold-toothed smile. "Don't make me laugh, Hardy!" he jeered. But at this moment a siren wailed outside.

"The cops!" gasped the surgical aide. "Let's blow!"

"Not till I take care of these three rats!" Grafton snarled. He started toward the detective and his sons, but Lemuel grabbed his sleeve frantically.

"Don't be a sap! We don't want a stretch in prison!"

As Doc's gaze shifted for a moment to Lemuel, Fenton Hardy snatched up a wet towel and hurled it at Grafton. It caught the criminal in the face and chest, checking his advance.

Lemuel and the others were already dashing from the room. Before Grafton could regain his wits, two more towels caught him in the face. Joe brought him down with a flying tackle and Frank pinned his arms.

While the two boys quickly subdued Grafton, Mr. Hardy raced in pursuit of the other criminals. They were running out the front door when they blundered straight into the arms of Chief Collig and a trio of husky policemen!

In a few minutes the fight was over. Doc Grafton and his cohorts stood panting and handcuffed, facing the Hardys and the police.

"How did you get here so fast?" Joe asked the burly chief.

"Well, for one thing, your father radioed us to stand by," Collig replied.

"That was right after I heard from you fellows," Mr. Hardy explained. "I figured the case was about to blow wide open, and as soon as I had the evidence, it would be time for Chief Collig to take over." He added that he had been seized by Lemuel and Sinder soon after entering the building. Upon close examination the men had recognized the detective's features.

"Then we got a second call from Chet Morton to get here in a hurry," Collig told the boys. "He contacted us over your car radio." The chief turned as Chet himself came bustling in through the front door. Frank and Joe pounced on him joyfully with bear hugs and handshakes.

"I'm glad you're okay!" Frank exclaimed.

"Chet, old buddy, you're the greatest!" Joe told him.

"I'm glad you fellows realize it," their chum said, his moonface splitting into a wide grin.

"Incidentally, we caught Nick Cordoza tonight and he talked plenty," Collig went on. "Seems he was a member of the Goggler gang—or the Evil Eyes, as they call it—and Malcolm Izmir was the head. Izmir had also been acting as banker for the gang's loot. But suddenly he told them it was time to break up—and then double-crossed them by paying them off in counterfeit money. No wonder they were trying to get him!"

Collig was astounded as the boys told him how Izmir had been picked up at sea by Lemuel and brought back to hide out at the health farm and have his face altered by Dr. Vardar.

"You two were way ahead of us," the chief commented wryly to the boys. "But that was a great job of detection, Frank and Joe. And you helped a lot, Chet."

A search was made of the building and half a dozen wanted criminals were taken into custody. All had been staying at the health farm—unknown to the regular guests—and were in process of recovering from facial surgery. The patient whom Frank and Joe had seen on the operating table turned out to be Pampton.

A figurine found in Izmir's money belt was indeed the Jeweled Siva. Also secreted, in other waterproof pouches, were diamonds and thousand-dollar bills.

Glumly the captured ringleader told his story. Lemuel, whose help he needed to stage his fake drowning at sea, was the only member of the gang not included in the double cross. Doc Grafton, Sinder, and the surgical aide—an ex-convict named Frosh who had worked as a prison orderly —knew all about the Evil Eyes and Izmir's plan. He had promised them fat sums for their services.

"Some of the mob found out who I really was," Izmir said, "and my business investments were about to collapse. That's why I had to clear out. I figured I could start a new life with a new name and a new face."

"And become a figure in hiding," Frank remarked.

Izmir said that before sailing he had converted all his remaining funds into cash and diamonds. He had learned through Fontana about the Jeweled Siva being for sale and had concocted a scheme with the art dealer to get hold of it through a fake robbery.

"I paid Fontana with a new car," Izmir went on, "and he was also going to keep the insurance payoff for the theft. He lied to Mrs. Lunberry that his insurance didn't cover it."

All members of the gang possessed glass-eye receivers. Izmir had had them made in Japan as a means of signaling instructions to his men on criminal jobs. But Spotty Lemuel had dropped his glass eye aboard the *Sea Spook* and had returned to the boathouse to inquire about it.

"So Spotty did overhear Bill Braxton talking to us on the phone and knocked him out," Frank put in.

"Yes." Izmir went on to say that Lemuel had then guessed that the Hardy boys had become suspicious of him. Unable to find the eye after a frantic search, he realized it must be in the Hardys' possession.

This had thrown Izmir into a panic. He feared the boys or their father might foil his scheme to jump off the *Cristobal* with an inflatable life raft by picking up his radio signals once overboard. Frantic efforts had been made to get back the glass eye before he sailed—first by luring the boys into the ambush at the vacant house, later by having Frosh, disguised as a meter reader, attempt to crack the Hardys' safe. Finally he had tried the midnight summons to Lookout Hill.

Rip Sinder and Doc Grafton had assisted Lemuel at the Lookout Hill rendezvous while Frosh had decoyed Mrs. Hardy and Aunt Gertrude into leaving the house in order to blow open the safe.

After learning that one of the double-crossed gang members had held up the Bijou in a car stolen from Izmir Motors, Malcolm Izmir had come to keep watch on the police's activities near the crash scene. While there, he had spotted the Hardy boys, trailed them to Mrs. Lunberry's home, and left the warning sign chalked under her window. Fontana had reported the Hardys' attempt to talk to Zatta and this had led to the peddler's kidnapping.

Izmir guessed that the boys might trace the green sedan and had had a fake call made to his sales manager so that Sykes would get rid of them. Izmir himself had been in the automobile show-room that day and had spotted the boys approaching. He had left by a rear door, and later had had Lemuel and Sinder lure them into the road trap.

Hoping for a lighter sentence, Izmir willingly identified all members of the Evil Eye gang. Two of them were the men who had tried to break into his estate.

"We should be able to round up the rest of them without too much trouble," Collig said. "And that art dealer, Fontana, too."

Mr. Hardy accompanied the police and their prisoners to headquarters. Frank and Joe, with Chet, drove off in their convertible. As they passed through the arched gateway, Joe remarked, "Boy, it sure was lucky we got the juice to the fence switched off in time!"

"Juice? What do you mean?" Chet queried.

When their stout friend learned of his narrow

escape from the electrified fence, Chet's face went white. "You mean . . . you mean . . ." He gulped and slumped back on the seat.

"Good grief! Chet's fainted!" Joe cried out.

Frank winked and said sadly, "Too bad Chet had to pass out. I was all set to buy him all the banana splits he could put away."

Chet's eyes opened and he sat up indignantly. "Well, for Pete's sake, why didn't you say so?" he complained.

Joe grinned. "No more rugged diets, eh pal?"

"You said it! And no more getting mixed up in any dangerous Hardy cases!"

But this resolution of Chet's was soon to be forgotten when Frank and Joe were confronted with **THE SECRET WARNING.**

"Come on!" Chet urged. "My mouth's dry as cotton. Let's get over to the Hot Rocket!"

ORDER FORM

HARDY BOYS MYSTERY SERIES

Now that you've seen Frank and Joe Hardy in action, we're sure
you'll want to read more thrilling Hardy Boys adventures. To make
it easy for you to purchase other books in this exciting series, we've
enclosed this handy order form.

54 TITLES AT YOUR BOOKSELLER
OR COMPLETE AND MAIL THIS
HANDY COUPON TO:

GROSSET & DUNLAP, INC.
P.O. Box 941, Madison Square Post Office, New York, N.Y. 10010

Please send me the Hardy Boys Mystery and Adventure Book(s) checked below @
$1.95 each, plus 25¢ *per book* postage and handling. My check or money order
for $_____ is enclosed.

1.	Tower Treasure	8901-7	27.	Secret of Skull Mountain	8927-0
2.	House on the Cliff	8902-5	28.	The Sign of the Crooked Arrow	8928-9
3.	Secret of the Old Mill	8903-3	29.	The Secret of the Lost Tunnel	8929-7
4.	Missing Chums	8904-1	30.	Wailing Siren Mystery	8930-0
5.	Hunting for Hidden Gold	8905-X	31.	Secret of Wildcat Swamp	8931-9
6.	Shore Road Mystery	8906-8	32.	Crisscross Shadow	8932-7
7.	Secret of the Caves	8907-8	33.	The Yellow Feather Mystery	8933-5
8.	Mystery of Cabin Island	8908-4	34.	The Hooded Hawk Mystery	8934-3
9.	Great Airport Mystery	8909-2	35.	The Clue in the Embers	8935-1
10.	What Happened At Midnight	8910-6	36.	The Secrets of Pirates Hill	8936-X
11.	While the Clock Ticked	8911-4	37.	Ghost at Skeleton Rock	8937-8
12.	Footprints Under the Window	8912-2	38.	Mystery at Devil's Paw	8938-6
13.	Mark on the Door	8913-0	39.	Mystery of the Chinese Junk	8939-4
14.	Hidden Harbor Mystery	8914-9	40.	Mystery of the Desert Giant	8940-8
15.	Sinister Sign Post	8915-7	41.	Clue of the Screeching Owl	8941-6
16.	A Figure in Hiding	8916-5	42.	Viking Symbol Mystery	8942-4
17.	Secret Warning	8917-3	43.	Mystery of the Aztec Warrior	8943-2
18.	Twisted Claw	8918-1	44.	Haunted Fort	8944-0
19.	Disappearing Floor	8919-X	45.	Mystery of the Spiral Bridge	8945-9
20.	Mystery of the Flying Express	8920-3	46.	Secret Agent on Flight 101	8946-7
21.	The Clue of the Broken Blade	8921-1	47.	Mystery of the Whale Tattoo	8947-5
22.	The Flickering Torch Mystery	8922-X	48.	The Arctic Patrol Mystery	8948-3
23.	Melted Coins	8923-3	49.	The Bombay Boomerang	8949-1
24.	Short-Wave Mystery	8924-6	50.	Danger on Vampire Trail	8950-5
25.	Secret Panel	8925-4	51.	The Masked Monkey	8951-3
26.	The Phantom Freighter	8926-2	52.	The Shattered Helmet	8952-3
			53.	The Clue of the Hissing Serpent	8953-X
			54.	The Mysterious Caravan	8954-8

SHIP TO:

NAME
_____
(please print)

ADDRESS
_____

CITY _____ STATE _____ ZIP _____

☐ 16.